'Boom Shankar! The Other Shore is a rare gem of a book that speaks from the heart in ways that are both familiar and exotic. The text draws a reader into the universe of the 1960s and 70s mystical Indian travel experience—the so-called 'hippie trail'—using a timely narrative device that incorporates our current Covid-19 experience. It is a piece for the moment: complex, engrossing and eloquent, and laced with wry humour. I can't recommend it highly enough.'

Professor Matthew Allen
James Cook University

THE OTHER SHORE

STORYTELLER MICHAEL QUINN
ARTIST PHILLIP ASHMAN

Published in 2021 by World Storywaters.
www.facebook.com/worldstorywaters

Paperback ISBN: 978-0-6451918-0-6

~ *To Friendship* ~

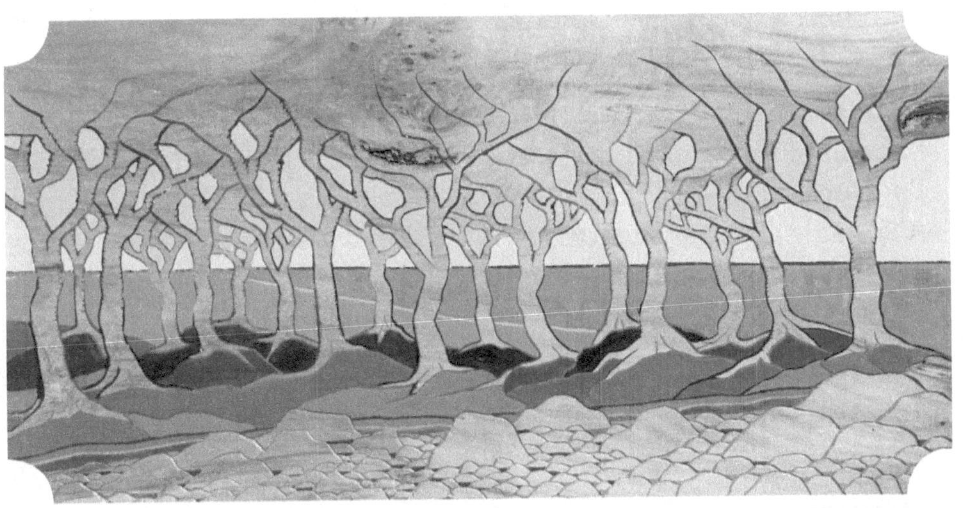

Step across the rocks,
cross the green between the dancing trees
gaze along the shore
to where land, sea and sky
vanish in infinity.

To find the world within a piece of wood
and eternity hour upon hour.

CONTENTS

CONTENTS

THE OTHER SHORE

We smoked more that night and the *Superior Person* went on and on that this world we perceived was not the world but our own socially constructed fiction about it. That it was all in our heads: *Maya*, illusion! That we had to wake up to *Bodhi consciousness*.

You let him rave on and on, until the sound of a cockerel crowing made us realise it was nearly dawn. You started making tea and porridge. More of our supplies would feed our freeloader.

Sometimes I wished you wouldn't leave these executive decisions to me. It all got too much for me so I told him to cultivate his own garden and not presume that we were spiritual novices. I told him to stop freeloading and leave.

He got up immediately and said, *I leave you with my Maya*, grabbed his bag and was out the door but not before launching a gob of spit at the wall and saying *Shu!* The saliva hung there in the flickering light of the candle. Then he was gone. Or should I say, *Thus gone?*

The candle flickered out.

Does memory go back from here
a recollection of the already known
or come here from there
an eruption from the past?
Is this life when looked back on
like a palimpsest?
Certain images show through,
from the past to the present
like the light from long dead stars.

DAY TWENTY-NINE

Captive Audience

Ground control to Major Tom. Hey man! It's me, Sam.

I'm talking to you from your tomorrow and here you are floating in a coma in a National Health Service intensive care tin can. You look like a cosmonaut in cryogenic suspension on a trip between worlds.

I don't know if you can hear me or sense my virtual presence, but the doctor told me to try talking to you as if you were conscious and not in some black hole at the centre of the Milky Way. She tells me that if coma patients hear familiar voices talking about the past, they might come back to consciousness. As it happens, I've been looking into our times together, so instead of sour grapes for your bedside table I've got a bunch of stories for you.

It's amazing. I'm looking at you in your hospital bed in Scotland, from my veranda in Kuranda. We were sitting out here together three years ago. Talking to you like this feels kind of silly. It's like talking into the void. I wish you'd twitch a finger or a toe, or blink open your eyes. Wake up!

You won't believe what's happened since you've been comatose. I can understand you staying where you are. Out of this world. If you come back, you'll get a real shock. Incredible. Fifty years ago, we could never have imagined this future. It's verging on apocalyptic.

No wonder I've been depressed. Everything is topsy-turvy, the whole world: ice-sheets are melting at the poles, Himalayan glaciers in meltdown, forests burning everywhere and still there are those who call global warming "fake news". There are wars and streams of refugees and now a viral pandemic and a noxious tide of conspiracy theories and infomania.

Fifty years ago, we travelled far from England to escape the Machine and now, ironically, you are being kept alive by the machinery of life-support flashing and beeping around you. Your sons have been in touch with me and have arranged with the hospital to allow me to talk to you at this time every day or, in your case, night.

Look man, I'm raising a whisky glass to you. Slange.

Thank you, yes, Slange var.

If you open your eyes and look into the screen facing you, you'll see me and the sun rising over the rainforest. These new phones, man, they're magic. The idea was pure sci-fi back when we were young. Now, everywhere you go you see people with their heads down over their mobile oracle. Plato's vision of the cave realised, made manifest. Now everyone is in their own cave watching their own screen and believing in the reality it represents, cut off from the living world.

If you open your ears, you'll hear not only me, but butcher birds, friar birds, catbirds, kookaburras and there goes the raucous sulphur-crested white cockatoo. Remember, I told you the names of these birds in the ancient lingo of this place. The people say the birds are ancestral spirits bringing messages to those with ears to hear. The cicadas and frogs provide a ceaseless background chorus, an underlying shrill. It's the eternal Dreamtime calling out.

The hospital is recording this conversation and they will play parts to you in an attempt to bring you back from wherever you are. It's on a loop. To escape the loop, you have to wake up, but I warn you it's not the same world you left. Everyone everywhere in lock-down. A liminal state. The world's in limbo and so are you. We once blessed people who sneezed, now we wish the devil would take them. No kisses, no hugs, no hand shaking! You'll have a hard time coping. New behaviours you'll have to adjust to like social-distancing and constant handwashing like Lady Macbeth.

No traffic on the road. Empty streets. No flights. Empty skies. Silence.

The Machine has stopped.

Well not entirely. I'm still able to communicate with you and you are monitored, fed, hydrated, and have your wastes extracted by the Machine. Not the best conditions for communicating but even if I were in Scotland, I wouldn't be allowed in your physical presence because of the virus.

Carpe Diem! I say to myself each day.

Dr Pendrill, who is treating me for my depression, has told me I need to find purpose in my life as a way of overcoming my death-wish, manifested in my "addictive behaviours". You have given me that sense of purpose. In fact, far from feeling depressed, I'm feeling decidedly merry. It's like this quest to speak with you is opening doors in my memory, leading me back to the times we shared and a Nietzschean re-evaluation of all values! Ha-ha!

I wish we could share this pipe, man. Boom Shankar! All hail to Shiva! Shiva's drug of choice.

Over all the years we've known each other, whenever we met up, we've reminisced, trying to articulate the wonder of those days. You are the pharmakon, the poison that is the cure. You have given me a hero's quest. A reason for being.

You were found sitting in the lotus position in your walled garden, beneath that datura plant with its angel's trumpets hanging over your head. I remember you told me you like to sniff its psycho-active blooms. *Too much!* I warned you back then.

At first, they thought you were dead, there were no perceptible vital signs. But you were in a coma.

Your sons are hoping that I'll bring you back from whatever mental state you've travelled to between life and death. I've still got that book you gave me by that monk you met at Samye Ling Monastery. *The Tibetan Book of the Dead.* Maybe you are in the *Bardo*!

I know you're not dead yet, but here you are in the gap between living and dying. That's the Bardo too. Not just the space between lives, which lasts forty-nine days. I'm trying to ease your consciousness in the right direction through talking to you. It's called, "Liberation in the Intermediate State through Hearing". Don't want you to suffer in hell or become a hungry ghost driven by insatiable craving, or become an animal or a demi-god, even a god. Even though I know you are inclined that way.

According to your boys, you've already been in a coma for twenty-nine days. You've either got to come back now or go through it all again. Be born again. Trapped in a new samsara web. Let me liberate you from your Bardo, so listen up!

Sol sent me a packet of old photos he discovered in your house. He thought they might bring back some memories of our time in India. Remember, we were going to sell our tale to the newspapers and they said the pics were not good enough. Now, decades later they turn up again, still looking like shit, but ancient shit. I like them. They've got a weird timeless quality about them.

Sky emailed me shots of your woodcarvings. I've never told you what your art means to me. You always say that you think in images, whilst I'm blinkered by words. As I look at your work, I wonder if you are lost in some dark wood of the mind. Perhaps I can perceive what you are saying written in the grain. Perhaps my critique will help bring you back.

Once you told me that after I had left you without a rupee in Goa, you wandered around getting sun-stroke.

People thought you were crazy. You went into a forest for two weeks trying to find reality, to see beyond our own assumptions.

Ever since then it seems to me you've been revealing what you found.

Over the last fifty winters
you have looked deep into pieces of wood
and released your inner vision
with the work of knife and chisel.

I see this work as your song of innocence and experience. A golden youth on the left panel appears to be walking into the forest with his back to the viewer; on the other panel a dying god, arms outstretched, bound to the branches of the tree. A god of rebirth and regeneration perhaps. But my vision is theory-laden, blinkered. When I refocus, I wonder if the youth is priapic. My eye is tricked into seeing a face in what should be the back of a head. The figure now seems to be walking towards me, emerging from the forest with an erection. Now the figure on the right panel appears to be a woman, or a dryad who has fallen for the charms of the golden youth. Or is she that chick you met at a festival? Tamsin ... Theresa ... Pussy Willow?

But all these notions are my projections. I was hallucinating and my eye tried to make sense of it, impose order on chaos. Now I see the youth is following a path into the forest. Dying god? Wood nymph? Vanished into the treescape or back into my head. It's a wonder you didn't wake up on hearing my critique and leap onto your soapbox. You hate amateur psychologists and art critics with a passion. You are PASHMAN. That's how you sign off.

If you don't come back, the art world will never know the truth, but remain like me, lost in conjectures. If you do come back, I'd like you to meet my shrink. She might be able to sort you out. She likes a good headcase.

Dr H Pendrill knows more about me than she's letting on. When I asked her what the H in her name stood for, she said that our relationship was purely professional and that as a client I had no need to know. *I am sure I met her a long time ago*, but she said that's what all her aging male patients say. She's been instrumental in fixing this arrangement with your hospital and weaving our lives back together. Even if you are off-planet!

Soon I'll have finished my course of therapy and have no reason to see her. I want Dr P to find in me a suitable case for extended treatment. I want to be her number one case study. She's obviously interested in the outcome of my communications with you. So as long as you stay in a coma, I keep getting to see her. Sounds a bit selfish putting it like that, but in my shoes I'm sure you'd feel the same.

I'm the voice echoing in your comatose ears. It's like talking to an empty room or a wall, but I've come prepared, no chance I'm going to corpse it. I've been writing a book called *The Other Shore* all about our journey to the east. It's a coming of age story that's taken half a century to write. This writing activity is part of my therapy. Doctor Pen-drill is aptly named. She has a thing about one's life-narrative. Apparently, we all have one. It's the story we tell ourselves about who we are and the life experience that defines us from one another. She pointed out to me that each of us is born into a world of stories which shape us as characters in the emerging tale of our own lives.

According to her, the first casualty of this narrative compulsion is truth. We are a species of storytellers. Our fate is determined by the stories we tell each other and the fictions we confuse with reality. Our notions of the real are always based on just another story. Some stories are therapeutic and life-enhancing, whilst others are the 'mind-forged manacles' that enchain us and make us prisoners of our own beliefs and social systems.

She believes that in some cases it's possible to tweak the tale, release ourselves from its gravity and, in my case, exorcise the Black Dog. She has encouraged me to write and share with you my prose and poetry, my changing narrative viewpoints, and my post-modernist contempt for linear time and a coherent plot. You are my captive audience. The perfect listener, or not. You always said I liked the sound of my own voice.

It seems more than mere coincidence that Dr Pendrill had me reach back in my memory to the time you and I travelled to India. I've nick-named her Mnemosyne. Memory, Mother of the Muses. I've come to fancy the mysterious Dr Pendrill, but she says it's a case of 'transference'. I've transferred to her unsatisfied desire from my past unfulfilled attachments. She's probably right. *But I'm sure I've met her before somewhere.*

She's fascinated by the journal I kept of those times and is making me compare my present-day memories to what is actually revealed in its pages. You remember my black book. You had a white one for your sketches. My All-weather notebook has the words THE MAGIC KITE on its inside page in red felt-tip with the illustration of a sun partially obscured by clouds from which rain falls. Above this is written the legend COMING BACK (TO ME) AS THE BEYOND SLOWLY UNFOLDS. Perhaps, as in a sentence, meaning is always retrospective. You have to reach its end before its sense is re-collected.

I wrote this on the first page some months into the journey, making the journal into a palimpsest. I was retrospectively attempting to turn our trip into a fairy tale entitled the *Magic Sun Kyte.* Before long it was hard to distinguish what was actually happening from the unfolding fable. In the fable you were called Li Ho, a Chinese Daedalus and I was Han Shan. For some obscure reason I had associated myself with the poet of Cold Mountain. Mushroom is in there too, that chick we met on the Zeebrugge ferry.

Magic Sun Kyte Lost

Somehow the Sun Kyte had broken free of the jungle and flew into days and nights, and the nights burst their seams, spilt over into new dawns, and tho' time appeared to pass Li Ho, Han and Mushroom changed but a little, growing old as they grew young. At times, and these were usually moments when the moon was waning and the skies clouded, the Kyte hardly made any progress at all and the shapes of mountains, lakes and forests, cities, towns, streets and houses would loom menacingly about them.

And then, after five days and nights (which seemed but a few moments to Han) the Kyte flew into darkness that swelled around them. The Kyte sped less and less and finally plunged to earth with such a shock that Han, Li Ho and Mushroom were thrown clear. Han picked himself up from the ground, a bit shaken and looked around for his friends. Li Ho had found some matches and lit a fire and soon the three were standing together. But the Magic Kyte had vanished and there was confusion in their minds. Mushroom lay with Han and Li Ho slept, wrapt in a blanket unto himself.

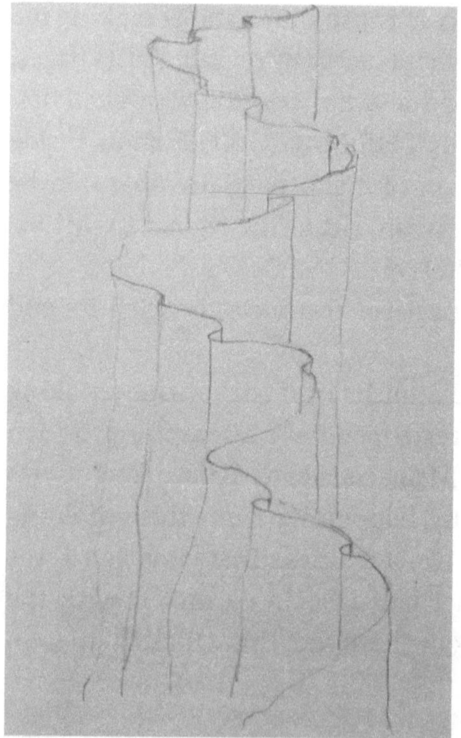

When daylight came Mushroom took the road west and Li Ho and Han set their faces towards the rising sun although it was obscured by clouds.

Li Ho kept a white book and made designs and words to go with them. He did not know why or where the pictures came from, but he saw that it was good. He was flying the Magic Kyte of his imagination.

But Han grew slip-shod in writing the story in his black book. He did not see what was to be seen nor hear what was to be heard. He had no idea what to say. Winter had fallen on the land and discontent sown in his soul.

The kite that inspired the tale was the one you had constructed at Portmeirion. A rather cumbersome affair that weighed quite a bit but took to the air with such gusto we both had to grab hold of its unspooling line. Then dramatically it halted in mid-flight and plunged towards us giving us a nasty scare before crumpling into the sand at our feet with an explosive snapping of its struts.

A year after our return from India when we were living at that commune on the Black Isle, I was sent on a mission to London to procure some vital necessities. I met a woman on Clapham Common. Children were flying kites. It was her first time out alone after her son was born and I walked up to ask her directions. She knew exactly what I wanted!

She had a copy of the I Ching and I did a reading for her. It told her to go to the north-west and Cross the Great Water. Her long red hair and flowing skirt reminded me of Pre-Raphaelite beauties. Her name, *Helene* means, *light, bright, shining* from Ancient Greek. I persuaded her to visit me. I lived in the north-west and the Great Water was just the ferry ride from Largs to the Black Isle.

Synchronicity! It was meant to be! We were destined to marry.

Six years later we returned to India with our young family. I had a thousand copies of *The Magic Sun Kyte* printed at our expense in Panjim, Goa. I hoped it would walk off the shelves in all good bookshops. I did find it in one such shop in London. It was there next to *Confessions of an English Opium-Eater*, by Thomas De Quincey. I took it as a sign of fame and fortune waiting just around the corner. Helene later promised that she'd put the unsold volumes in my coffin. But I'm sure she was joking. Could I really have been so wrapped up in my creative project as to have ignored its effects on my family's life?

The journal I had written of our journey to the East contained the seeds of future creation and romance. There's a dream in it about a young woman whose bags I'd carried as a porter at Portmeirion. In the dream I'd taken her to the *camera obscura* overlooking the estuary and revealed the world to her in a reflecting bowl. After recording the dream in my journal, I didn't think of her anymore. Thirty years later and single again, I was at a friend's house. He had just returned from filming on the Great Wall of China. He had a photo of himself standing there with his casting director, whose gamine looks seemed somehow familiar. The phone rang and it was her. As he got off the phone, he mentioned her name, *Elle*. Her identity was suddenly revealed as if in a reflecting bowl, so to speak. He gave me her number and I called. "Synchronicity!" we gasped and got married.

I've come to accept that the seeds of the future are planted deep in the past. My black journal addresses a future self with enigmatic sentences like the following:

From here to there is no distance, but you might change on the way.

I believe that was one of your inspirational sayings. I'm sure you said those words to me about the future. It's like you're talking to me now. Those words have been lying in the book half a century waiting to spring to my eyeballs. As I look back from the Age of Corona, I see much that is hidden in there. It is a mystery novel waiting fifty years for its denouement. There are tales nestling in tales like matryoshka dolls.

DAY THIRTY

Hello, hello, hello. What have we here? A man in a coma for thirty days. It's you, man. Time to return to the land of the living. Open your eyes and check out the view from my veranda. You loved the rainforest. Remember the supplejack and wait-a-while reaching their way from the ground to the canopy and strangler figs sending their roots down from above, strangling their helpless hosts. Remember the feeling of walking into the forest. For me, it's being enveloped within a living entity, with its buttress roots and mighty columns of tree trunks, its over-arching leafy canopies, the archetypal cathedral, nature's own. Its angels are the fig-birds, parrots and catbirds. Listen now! That's Daboy, the shrike thrush, the Doo-di-doo-di bird. I love her song, it seems to follow me whenever I go in the forest. Sometimes I think she's luring me deeper inside its vastness to get me lost.

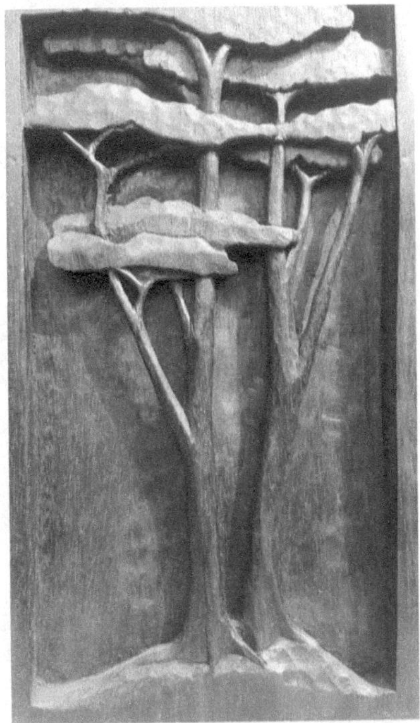

In the forest of your mind
you find your love
and side by side grow together
without a care
and drawing water through your roots
and poisons from the air
exhale the oxygen
for all life on earth to share.

Bags to Go Inside Bags

In the shack by the railway track in Goa you were making bags, and bags to fit inside the bags like those Russian dolls, nestling one inside the other, suggesting infinite recursion. I thought you were crazy. But now I see that you were planting in my consciousness the seeds of this story. We all have bags of memories and from each one another springs forth.

The Architect of Dreams

One night it is so hot that I leave you sleeping.

Outside comes the shush of palm leaves, like a shower of rain. The moon is waning but still strong enough to light my path. The world is blue and even the gully is bright. *Beware of snakes!*

I go downwind of the fishing village and their dog-pack. I'd heard that a traveller up north had been bitten and developed rabies.

One boat is at sea and another at my side is humped with nets and more nets are stretched out along the sands.

The breakers are swollen with the moon's power and billow luminous, then collapse like empty sails.

I sleep but am aware of the men coming to launch the boat.

Then I dream that it is daylight and I am lying in the same place on the beach. I become aware of a distant grumbling, getting ever closer and see a man on a motorbike surging towards me. He suddenly pulls up, showering me with sand and towers over me like a bearded genie in a turban, his machine gunning and growling.

Where are you coming from? What are you doing? Where are you going?

I try to jump up to get on a level with my aggressive inquisitor who suddenly evaporates. I find myself sitting up in the blue moon light, surrounded by growling dogs. I start laughing and the dogs wag their tails, give me some rabid licks and head off.

I give thanks to the Architect of Dreams who had turned me into a David facing Goliath and prepared me to face an overwhelming threat. I appreciated the bathos of the situation. It was a lucky dream by the Arabian Sea.

As the dogs leave, I notice the moon and morning star over the western horizon and fall asleep till dawn.

There are scratchy clouds in a raw sky into which the blue is running. To the north and to the south along the beach mists are rising.

A fisherman approaches me warily and I give him a *beedi*. The women then come and surround me and ask *What are you doing?* One of them picks up my bag and asks *What is in the bag?*

Instinctively I make a snaky motion with my hand and say *Snake!* She drops the bag and they all stand back.

To reassure them I empty my bag. There is nothing in my bag but a small leather purse containing a piece of driftwood, a tiger-striped shell, a broken watch, a silver sixpence on a ring, a piece of Tibetan coral and an ivory laughing Buddha. I display the contents on my sleeping mat.

One of the fisher people calls me a *sadhu* and another cries out *Magic!*

I leave the people and walk towards the sea.

Covered in sand is a sea snake that looks dead. I return it to the sea on the end of my stick and see its rainbow colours as the sand washes away. It returns to life with an energetic flicker of its body and is gone.

From behind I hear cries: *Magic! Magic! You have magic with snake. Don't lie!*

The Architect of Dreams was clearly still at work.

Feeling like a comic book castaway masquerading as a witch doctor, I let them lead me to their camp. They forgive me when I accidentally step on someone's shadow. They treat me to a breakfast of prawns, fish and rice. The camp dogs lick the salt on my feet.

Ouroboros

Because I've quoted you extensively in my black book, it is a record of our dialogue together. It's like a message in a bottle we wrote to future selves and cast into the sea from the eternal shore of Colva Beach, Goa. It has drifted on ocean currents for fifty years before washing up on the west coast of Scotland.

Through my therapy I've become aware that, unconsciously, I have been editing my memories for the sake of a story to enhance my own life-narrative, leaving out uncomfortable bits. This process of expanded awareness has been paradoxically therapeutic.

By examining the journal, I discover that some of my memories do not agree with the entries I made. I left out plenty of "uncomfortable bits" too. And it's full of things you said to me, even your dreams. Little did we realise that we'd be revisiting those times over and over again in our lives as if we were caught up in an eternal loop.

Once I recall asking you about that time in Afghanistan, you'd lost your passport and didn't care, because you were so stoned. How you'd walked up to this ancient castle with a sentry at the gate and walked right inside. You found yourself in a courtyard and as your eyes adjusted to the gloom, you saw squatting Afghans in manacles. You had walked into a prison. In this moment of illumination whistles blew and sentries descended from the ramparts with antique rifles aimed at you.

You told me it never happened to you and I didn't believe you.

Well, in the journal I discovered that you were right. It didn't happen to you. It happened to Fearless Freddy. He'd been following us in a Citroen all the way from Istanbul. But I can clearly see those squatting figures in their shackles. I reckon I was there with Freddy. I was the one who was stoned out of his mind.

To think that I had been recounting the tale about you to others, as if it was gospel. Deceived by my own memory. I was in denial. But it is true you had lost your passport and were blissfully without a care. We both were.

We both lived through the same experiences but sometimes have contradictory memories. If we can't agree about the true nature of our own experience, then what hope for history? We talked about this: how history was always a construct, shutting out other voices.

I'm hoping you'll come back to this world and refute my account, because if you don't, there's no one else who can, and I'll be forced to believe my own history. It's all in my head. Maybe that's all we can ever know—our consciousness, ever-looping into the past through memory and back again to the never-ending present moment, eating up the future as it devours the past like a snake with its tail in its mouth.

Today I'll leave you with a poem I wrote about the first time I saw you.

The Call of the Wild

Looking back in time
half a century
through memory's eye,
its crystal ball,
crossing a bridge between
then and now
here and there,
takes no time at all.

But *then* I lacked the words
that I say *now*
in this moonlight
with hindsight.

I saw you first in a college
for young Christian
ladies and gentlemen.
That was its flawed assumption.

You looked out of place
like you'd arrived from Deep Space
a fierce frown upon your face,
an angry bodhisattva
amidst a throng of dreamers
lost in *maya*, lost in sleep.

You looked anomalous
as a fox in a chicken coop
or a wolf in a flock of sheep.

You wore a halo of red gold hair
but looked like no saint.

You weren't even a Catholic!

You had a wild streak
artistic
iconoclastic
like a tear in the social fabric,
an *enfant terrible* of the *avant-garde,*
the child of a Blake or a Dali or Pablo Picasso
embodying a critique, a manifesto
woven of parody, satire,
& irony's caress
to wake up
human consciousness.

With flair you wore a sporting blazer,
tartan trews and two odd shoes.
Not seeking to impress
without a care you broke
all the codes of dress.

In that crowd of fashion and conformity
I'm sure you didn't see me passing by.
I was trying to look like a beatnik
but I knew I looked square
with my short-back-n-sides,
St Michael's crew neck jumper
and the grey schoolboy trousers
I was made to wear.

I had no idea
I'd just seen Destiny
sitting in a chair.

I had no crystal ball.
I was following
a red-headed Polish girl
in a mini skirt
down the corridor
in a cloud of menthol cigarette
and pheromones
to the lecture hall.

Now is always moving on, making the future the past. There is only the eternal present. Our unfolding lives are carried within it. Please come back. You are missing out. This is our chance to experience eternal life. You'll be a long time dead. Wake up.

DAY THIRTY-ONE

G'day me old mate. How's the Bardo going on day thirty-one? I expect you've already been picked up by a great wind, blown over lands and seas and left in a deep forest. According to the Tibetan Book of the Dead, all your present experiences are your own projections. Have no fear if the Lord of Death cuts off your head, severs your limbs, tears out your heart. Know that you will come to no harm. Just relax and go with the flow, man. Don't let your imagination run away with you. Gods? Demons? You're the one who quoted William Blake, "Thus man forgot that all deities reside in the human breast". That's my cold comfort for the day. Think of it as another bad trip with awful hallucinations. It will end. You will wake up to a new day.

Remember when I called myself Sam? No-one else would. It was when we first met, fifty years ago.

Salmon of Knowledge

In a fish and chip shop
we chanced to meet
not realising
we'd made a quantum leap
like sub-atomic particles suddenly colliding —
as fat was spitting in the deep fryer.

From yesterday's paper we ate the fare
with a sprinkling of salt n' vinegar.

The Moortown bus went one way
and the Roundhay bus the other.

I can't recall what we had to say
It didn't seem to matter.

If we'd eaten of the Salmon of Knowledge
crumbed, grilled or battered
and seen what was to come
the road to the East and back again
we could have altered history
taught in Huddersfield or Harrogate
and now been on a pension.

We could have been
so respectable
the very pillars of convention
played golf or bowls
and been a member
of the neighbourhood watch
ever vigilant
ever wary of the stranger.

We could have lived very different lives.

I didn't know that
I held one half of a map
and you held the other.

We were in a labyrinth of Fate's devising
and needed each other to find the way out.

We just licked our salty fingers
and wished each other goodnight
not realising our fate was sealed
that we'd already heard
the Song of the Open Road
and felt it like a call from deep inside
the Call of the Wild.

I was trying to become somebody. I'd given myself a new name to dissociate myself from my past and celebrate a new beginning. It was a phase I was going through. I thought it sounded strong and dependable. It could've been worse. It could've been *Treebeard*, but I had hardly a hair on my chin.

I wore an owl's feather in my hat and my Aunt Edna's fur coat with chopped-off sleeves, so it hung like a cloak.

We set out on a quest to find our *selves*. In those days we believed that our *selves* were out there somewhere waiting for us to find them and that if *we did our own thing* some day we'd meet up and become that *self*. A bit like going looking for your glasses when they're sitting on your head, which I do a lot of these days, even when I've got a pair in each hand.

I'm just gabbling to you. We never consciously set out to find ourselves, that was just the accepted wisdom of the time. It's more a case of our *selves* finding *us*, after becoming who *we are* through the processes of time.

I'm Not a Number, I'm a Free Man

In 1968
at weekends
from Trinity and All Saints we'd escape,
each travelling by thumb
to Scarborough or the Lakes
and meeting up again, sleep rough
with a groundsheet and a sleeping bag
in bus-shelter or graveyard
in sea-front pavilion or lakeside glade
eating fish 'n chips or baked beans from a can
sitting in a pub and drinking black and tan.

It felt like we were free.
Two rival princes on a quest
for a Rapunzel in a tower
or a Cinderella without a shoe
or a rich chick in a sports car
with only room for one
on the road to Timbuctoo.

We were we driven by
the Spirit of the Times
pulling all our strings
unconsciously.
The Incredible String Band.
The whole Zeitgeist.

We were being played by
Ginsberg, Kerouac and Leary,
the Beatles and the Maharishi,
Dylan, Donovan and Patrick McGowan,
a never-ending list.

We were rolling stones.
We were week-end beats.
We were prisoners on day-release.
We were not numbers.
We were seekers of *nirvana*
on the road again
looking for the Other Shore.

We travelled to Portmeirion
in midwinter and trespassed
sleeping in an empty hotel room
and escaping out the window at dawn
like *The Prisoner.*

We'd seen it on TV
and watched each week avidly
as if it held the key to our identity
and now we ran in his footsteps
along the estuary sand bar
crying out the mantra
exultantly

I'm not a number
I'm a free man.

Back then, we followed each other. Our parents thought we each were a bad influence on the other as we hitch-hiked here and there and smoked banana skins or harvested poppy heads from the neighbour's garden and paid little attention to our obligations as trainee teachers of future generations of young Catholic ladies and gentlemen.

Instead of joining a variety of Catholic associations like the Legion of Mary, we associated with Junkie Jonny who rolled twelve-inch joints with licorice paper, Capstan full-strength and Moroccan gold. I was the one who dropped out first and I had anxious moments that night wondering if you had decided to go straight, continue your education and abandon me. But we were equals. If I'd said let's go to the Skeleton Coast and pick up diamonds, you'd have followed me. You did, at times, manifest a voice of wisdom and initiate an on-going critique of who I think I am that has persisted for half a century.

Remember Helenka Jakubowska, that redhead I followed around at the college, love-struck. You had something going with her friend Lorraine. Well, Helenka came up in my therapy session with Dr Pendrill. I wrote an account of it for your pleasure. Dr P was going on about my pursuit of "limerent objects", unobtainable love objects, redheads who glimmered like red gold.

A Suitable Case for Treatment:
A Session with Mnemosyne

"I wonder, then", Dr Pendrill interjected, "was this the first of your long obsessions with an unobtainable love object? Or limerent object, I should say. It is common enough for unresolved attachment issues to manifest as limerence".

I was a little piqued at the suggestion that she thought me common, but I let her continue. "You have already told me about Helenka, the red-headed Polish girl and the vivid fantasies that accompanied any contact. I'm not surprised that her obvious disinterest fuelled your obsessive, intrusive thoughts".

As she spoke, I could picture Helenka again, a cloud of smoke following her along the hallway of the mezzanine floor of the campus, a gentle, lyrical cough shaking her long silky scarf of red-gold hair and the alabaster skin of the faint line of her cleavage.

I felt that old heartache of waiting for her to return my love, understanding that it may never happen. That first sinking feeling of hopelessness came the time I went to meet Helenka and her boyfriend in London, when I realised what a nice guy he was. The guilt cut deep. And anyway, I was thinking, "How could such a beautiful, fit and healthy goddess in her prime ever want me ...", when I became aware again of what Dr Pendrill was saying, "... always playing up the positive aspects of the limerent object and discounting or identifying with the negative aspects".

Her relentless gaze was pointedly fixed on my tobacco-stained fingers. I shifted in the leather armchair, which let out an awkward squeak as I sat on my hands. I had an overwhelming urge to light up a rollie, just so I could encase myself once more in Helenka's delicate parfum.

Dr Pendrill had shifted gear again, sitting forward meaningfully in her seat, "the restorative for the addictive personality is", she opened the chasm of one of her meaningful pauses, "to live a PURPOSEFUL LIFE", she added allowing a little more weight to the last two words, as if CAPS LOCK had been accidently turned on by the flick of her little finger adjusting her glasses. Her hand fell down to the pen on the coffee table next to her. She started writing on an official-looking form. I was pleased she was really listening and taking me seriously enough to take clinical notes. I must be a very interesting case. Unique even.

In fact, my FILE was written in her well-rounded handwriting that finished the letters e, g and o with strangely hooked flourishes. I had found that I could even make out some of what she was writing in the wall mirror behind her chair. It gave me the dizzying sensation of seeing my inner parts laid out backwards. For example, her comments on my description of Aunt Edna's sleeve-shorn fur coat and my hat with the pheasant feather noted that I was currently wearing a black felt top hat with a red-tailed black cockatoo feather, an ayahuasca-design waistcoat, a t-shirt with a Cretan labyrinth design and a standard non-fairtrade crystal pendant on a plaited thong.

I felt like an exhibit. That my personae over time had been caricatured. The veiled sarcasm undercut the front I present to the world. I was pinned like a bug for all to see. Exhibitionist tendency! Wannabe shaman!

I have to remind myself that I am not a drop in the ocean, but the entire ocean in a drop.

I can't help wondering what she thinks of you after I told her I associated you with a stellar cast of mystics and poets: Li Ho and Li Po, Han Shan's friend Shi-Te, William Blake and Rumi's mentor Shams.

I told her Rumi was a bookish scholar who in his late thirties met a wandering weaver of baskets, a poet, philosopher and teacher. I had just started saying, "Whose name was ...", when she interrupted and continued seamlessly, "Shams. It means the Sun. Shams believed he had found the right man to become his master student. The meeting was transformational. For Rumi, Shams shone as a guide to the right path, dispelling the darkness in his heart". She added, rather unnecessarily, I thought, "Yes, I can Google too". Then she went for one of her twists, "But what did Rumi and Shams mean to you?"

I told her you have always made me question my assumptions. You are like Shams dispelling the darkness. I explained that we often argued together over the primacy of visual imagery or words in the thought process, as if they were rivals and not bed-mates.

When I look into your art, I hear these words of Rumi echoing in my head: let the heart take over the conversation. No need for words or alphabet.

Dr Pendrill raised an eyebrow just a fraction when I started telling her that Shams had a nickname 'The Bird' because he travelled widely and had been known *to be in two places at the same time.* I could see in the mirror that her writing became slightly more fevered as I explained that you often appeared from nowhere, like from behind me on a bus going to Tewkesbury or sitting on the terrace beneath the Taj Mahal when I thought I'd seen the last of you in Delhi.

That day in Agra I had resisted the temptation to see the Taj but as the day wore on, I could not stop myself from joining the multitude walking towards it as the sun was setting. As I walked towards the marble monument to love, I spotted your blazing halo of red hair. You were sitting in the centre of a terrace with your back against a parapet immediately beneath the massive cupola of the Taj. You were at the centre of a mandala in a land of teeming millions. It's like I was being drawn towards you by some mystic force.

You must have taken this photograph minutes before I arrived.

Dr Pendrill was scribbling quite fast when I told her about setting out to find you in Goa. It only took three days. I had no idea where you might have disappeared to, but there you were in a chai shop in Calangute. You said you'd known I had arrived three days before, the very day I disembarked in Panjim. I had to admit to Dr P that it always felt spooky, as though we were telepathically connected in some way.

I tried to make my glances over to the mirror as casual-looking as possible. But when I read 'can be in two places at the same time' in the mirror-writing, I had a brief seizure of cognitive dissonance, having read it as 'can be in two times at the same place' before realising that this was impossible. There were also some jottings along the lines of 'bird symbolism, flight, reality avoidance, infantile belief, magical omnipotence, hyperinflation of the ego and Peter Pan complex'.

That's what I saw, man. You'd think I'd be ashamed, but I was thrilled. I wanted to be a suitable case for treatment.

DAY THIRTY-TWO

Hello from my veranda. Wake up please. If you are in the Bardo, pass from the darkness into the light. The experience of dissolving into the luminosity is supposed to be terrifying. Have no fear. Think of yourself as salt dissolving in water, just let go man!

Don't join the hungry ghosts! Free yourself from the Five Poisons, your confused emotions! Become the essence of what is!

Man, it is great to take over your soapbox! Now I'm in the pulpit for a change. But *less is more,* as you always say.

I've been telling Dr Pendrill stories about my mother. You remember Mom. You loved to provoke her. She thought you were the Antichrist leading me astray. She chased you out of the house once after you'd got on your soapbox and lectured her on morality being a relative affair, depending on where and whichever time you were born into. You really knew how to set her off! You told me later that you knew she loved you, and she did.

Under the Influence

Once upon a time when I was very young, I opened my parents' bedroom window and climbed onto the windowsill.

I was under the influence of Peter Pan.

The window looked out from the third floor over a park with woodlands and a stream crossed by stepping-stones and wooden bridges from which I played *Pooh sticks.*

My mother was lying sick in bed. She asked me what I was doing.

I told her I was only going to fly to my friend Andrew's house next door and knock on his bedroom window.

She suggested that I climb up on the bed and practise flying in the room before heading out the window.

Her wise maternal advice extended my life.

Hallucinations: Three Witches on Broomsticks

My bedroom was in the attic and had a skylight.

My favourite book was Rupert Bear. There were three witches and they flew on broomsticks across the sky. They were ugly and menacing but I loved looking at the illustration, finding a mysterious pleasure in horror.

One night my parents tucked me into bed, telling me that they were going to visit friends down the road and that Jack and June would look after me if I needed anything.

I fell asleep but woke up in the moonlight falling through the skylight. Looking up I saw three witches on broomsticks flying across the face of the moon.

I was already out of bed. I took giant steps down three flights of stairs to the hall and ran in my pyjamas crying down the street.

Happily, I found my parents and sobbed out my tale.

My mother returned to my bedroom with me and looked up at the night sky. She showed me scratches in the glass of the skylight and told me that my mind had turned the scratches into witches.

This came as an amazing relief.

Later in life when I see faces in trees or rocks, or in the clouds, it is a consolation to know that I am pareidolia prone and not to have a full-blown panic attack as a consequence.

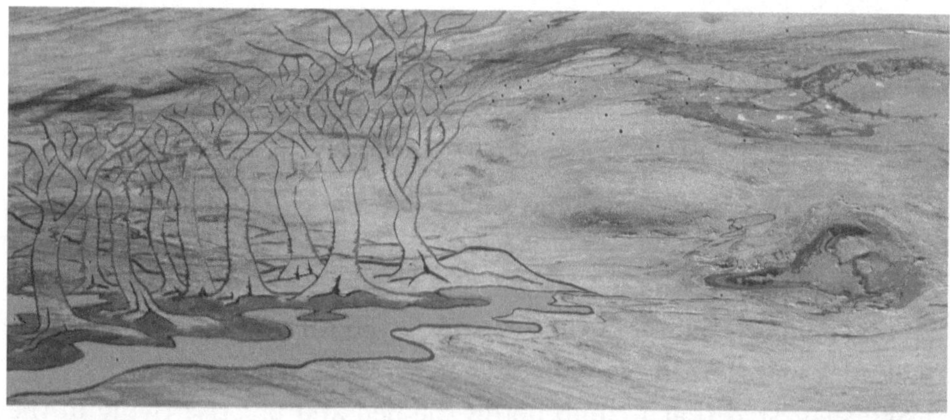

By looking into your art, I see that pareidolia has its way with you. I see the dryadic community embracing the heavens in a celebration of pure existence, transformational, not static. The Dance of Life. I've heard that imagination is a tree because it is capable of integrating earth and sky, reality and the ideal. I suspect you learned your art millennia ago in sacred caves: how to see visions suggested by the surface of the rock, its colouration, its texture and curvatures.

Art was always already a collaboration with the world, a response, an identification with something out there, beyond us. The idea embodied in pre-existing forms. The Word made Flesh. An ancient sage observed the world to be like the impression left by the telling of a story. I see that in your carving.

The burning forests of the Amazon
and the Australian bush
cried out to you
but you left a branch of hope.

I'll be back tomorrow at the same time.
Boom Shankar!

DAY THIRTY-THREE

Wake up! Wake up! That's the Masked Friarbird, talking in English.

It's me again. Hope you're receiving me, Major Tom.

Back to your Bardo. It's not only the gap between lives but the suspension of life in the living situation. Like you in your coma. You'll have to practise the ways of liberation: liberation through the ear. You can start by listening to me. Then there's liberation through the eye, the memory, touch and taste. These words I'm sending out to you might take the form of a strand of spider web that you can climb up back to this world.

Now the Butcherbird is calling out. Kalpoo! Kalpoo!

Yesterday I had a close encounter with Kalpoo. Taught me a lesson.

I'd gone into the bathroom and noticed a lizard stuck in the bath. He or she couldn't scale its sides. I thought I'd do a good deed and perform a rescue. As I released it on the windowsill, the lizard took its chance and passed under the louvre to the outside world.

BANG! Kalpoo struck the window and I watched aghast as it flew to a tree and banged the lizard's head against a branch, before gulping it down. My good deed had resulted in the death of the wee creature and lunch for my friend, Butcherbird.

It makes me question my motives for talking to you like this. Am I doing it to feel or look good? Are the stories I am telling you going round and round your head like the winking lights and chatterings of your life-support system? Are you stuck in an infernal loop? How much are you aware of?

You still look like you are off-planet, man. It's not a good look.

Not a good look here either. I've been sneaking out. It's like the end of the world. Empty streets with curlew sentinels. Mobs of birds in the fig trees. Bush turkeys emptying already empty bins. It's uncanny. No train, no Skyrail, no tourist coaches, no shops, no market. Nobody.

The only person I get to talk to is you and you are in a coma.

No comment.

I'll read you a chapter from *The Other Shore*. I know you'd laugh if you could.

Summer of Love

You will recall that halcyon summer, the *Summer of Love* when we dropped out of college and hit the road, ending up in Cornwall, washing dishes and peeling spuds in a restaurant in Newquay. You took over the washing-up because you said I was half-blind and left egg-stains on the plates and unknown debris in the prongs of forks. I did the drying without complaint. Washing dishes made the skin of the hands crinkle up in a rather repulsive way.

It was a great job. We had our eyes on a couple of waitresses, red-headed Lena and her friend Donna, who slept in a flat of their own. We slept in those brand-new drainage pipes outside the town, or in that church porch where the organist stepped over us in the morning to practice his Bach.

Once we left our gear in a cave on a rocky ledge and went for a pint in the local. You remember that guy at the bar who asked me who I was looking at? I happened to be gazing at his leggy, mini-skirted companion at the time and declared that I wasn't looking at anyone, just daydreaming. He told me to fuck off and daydream somewhere else. I complained to you that he was lacking in couth but you told me he was in his rights and that I had been staring at her with my tongue hanging out. When we got back to the beach, the tide was in and we had to wade into the dark cave to retrieve our sleeping bags and clothes from the ledge that fortunately was inches above the lapping waters.

We got sacked after we had taken a vow of silence, which the restaurant manager took for rank insubordination rather than an ascetic trial we had set ourselves for the sake of our spiritual development. That very night I lost my virginity with Lena the waitress. Well, I lost something. I had to make love in the presence of her friend Donna who was stifling her laughter in the dark and her doggy companion, a slobbery Boxer who wanted to join me in my efforts to satisfy his mistress.

The next morning, despite my exasperating amatory exploits, I felt that at last I was a man. It was a consolation to think you had to sleep rough, whilst I had been cosying up to the love (so far) of my life. That night, as if to mock me, you moved in with Donna, with no thought for the overcrowding, and made close friends with the Boxer. I had always been led to believe that you were sexually experienced and regarded you as my sexual guru. Years later you confessed that Donna was your first lover and that I had actually lost my virginity twenty-four hours before you.

Our interlude of pleasure ended in the morning when we were both evicted.

DAY THIRTY-THREE

DAY THIRTY-FOUR

Hello dear friend. It's me again with your wake-up call from Oz.

Hear the Kookaburras, greeting the day with bubbling laughter. Their message is not to take things too seriously. Feel the ecstasy of being throbbing through your body. Have a good laugh. They are telling you a visitor is on the way. That's me.

I've been trying to imagine you in the Bardo. How will you experience space without a body to relate to? Immersed in it like water in your whisky.

I've got my whisky. Slange.

Thank you, Slange var!

I'm enjoying being an art critic looking into your carvings and thinking up some entries to go into the catalogue for the auction of your surviving works, should you fail to come back to this world. I've told Sky and Sol we have to be realistic. There might be a bob or two to be made with your collection. I've suggested the title *DendroPhillia.* Hot hey! Sexy.

You see the World Tree in each block of wood,
the Tree of Life, the Tree of Knowledge,
the Tree of the Imaginary.
Your chisel frees the archetype.

I've been looking into your relationship with the Dryads. It seems rather intimate. That's a seller. The market will lap it up. Eros means dollars, pounds, euros, lucre, lots of it.

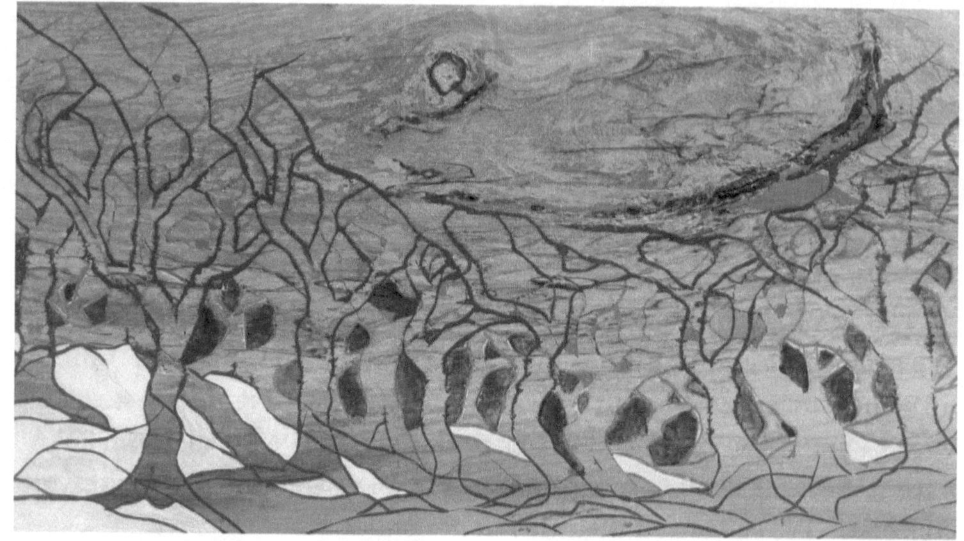

Orgasmic forest. Dance of the Dryads amidst snowy drifts.

Here's another episode from *The Other Shore*. I'm not sure if I ever told you the whole story.

A Job with Good Prospects

After dropping out of College and enjoying idyllic summer months on the road with you, I went home, happy to have lost my virginity in Newquay. My parents were quick to suggest that it was time I settled down and got a good job. I studied the Yorkshire Post's employment section and circled the first one that caught my eye.

The next morning, I caught a bus and arrived in the early morning mist that blanketed Holbeck Hill cemetery, my chosen workplace.

The shrouded cemetery with its Victorian tombs and funerary statuary resembled the setting of a gothic tale by Edgar Allan Poe.

The Superintendent, a sallow-faced individual, took me under his wing, seeming to favour me over all the others in the workforce, who, coincidentally, suffered from forms of epilepsy. Why the council employed epileptics as cemetery workers I had no idea. It became a common experience to hear cries coming from the mist as one or another of my co-workers succumbed to a fit. One morning I found Cedric thrashing about on the floor of a freshly-dug grave. The Super bravely descended into the grave to give first-aid but was kicked or kneed in his privates for his pains. Everyone tried not to laugh. Apparently during a seizure, the sufferer has no control over his actions, but some of the gang believed that the foot or knee had been launched intentionally.

After a funeral when all the mourners had departed, Cedric and Bertie (short for Ethelbert) would perform an archaic dance on the newly filled-in grave in their clay-cleated boots. I found time during the day to slip away from my tasks. I wandered through the cemetery, noting the names of each deceased, the dates of their birth and death, and any verses or sayings inscribed on the tombstones. Some lives ended virtually as soon as they started, others reached into old age. I often mused on the fact that I knew my own birthday but that final date was left to Fate. In my dreams I saw a giant chessboard on which people were the pieces: kings, queens, knights, bishops, pawns going through their paces, not knowing if they'd live or die, be taken or checkmated. The rich had their own tombs and mausoleums and marble angels whilst the poor lay crowded in common unmarked graves.

One day the Super took me aside and asked me how I was enjoying the job. I replied that I found it satisfying to work amongst the graves and greatly enjoyed the company of my fellow workers. The Super began to talk excitedly of the long-term benefits of being employed at Holbeck Hill. He took me to a plot and proudly declared it the site of his own future grave and that he had been allowed to choose it himself. This was one of the perks of employment at the cemetery. Young people should think about the future and practice long-term planning.

I nodded in agreement with the wisdom of the Super's words.

"You've got a great view from here", I said, unable to think of anything meaningful to say.

"That's why I chose it", said the Super.

Actually, I was not so happy with my employment. I could never get the cleats of clay off my boots and the smell of decay from my nose.

I had met a nice university student called Eleni who had been acting oddly with me after I'd told her where I was working. She had actually shouted at me when I had walked down her hallway and left a trail of "graveyard mud" on its carpet.

On the day I was offered a more permanent position in the graveyard, the side of a new grave fell away revealing a disintegrated coffin in the next plot. A common occurrence apparently. I had stared at the macabre scene and turned away in disgust as miasma filled my nostrils.

That night I dreamed that it was twilight and I was walking through the cemetery, engulfed in a thick mist. Ahead of me, I glimpsed my co-workers standing round a graveside. As I approached, they came forwards to block me from looking in the grave. Cedric and Bertie grabbed hold of me. I woke in fright, knowing it had been my own grave.

Another dream had the dead arising from their resting places, walking from their tombs. A multitudinous crowd of the dead milled through the cemetery. I had woken up not in exultation at the long-predicted resurrection but filled with dread.

I left the job after only six weeks.

The Super was disappointed. He'd had great expectations for my future at Holbeck Hill and promised that there'd always be a place for me there if I changed my mind. I didn't tell him I'd had a better offer. That I was upwardly mobile and had accepted the offer of employment as hotel porter at Portmeirion. My benefactor was none other than Sir Clough Williams-Ellis, the architect. We'd met him after trespassing in the village when the hotel was closed, and he'd taken a liking to us vagabonds. I didn't know that this was going to change my life and yours too.

You joined me there as a waiter. The spectral village with its many perspectives and *trompe l'oeil* lay before us. This place was in our hearts: Italianate architecture, towering camponile, magical pastel-coloured dwellings, its shrine to Buddha, its arches and colonnades, its ponds and mythical statuary. The wildwood the *gwyllt* as its backdrop and the magnificent estuary spread out before it.

Last image of your vanished masterpiece,
unveiled by Sam the porter in Portmeirion in 1969

We read *Steppenwolf* and, in our minds, we entered the Magic Theatre, courtesy of Herman Hesse; over the entrance was written FOR MADMEN ONLY. We saw a long corridor stretching without end before us. On either side were doors, each opening onto a unique realm of human experience. We were hungry for life. We wanted to open all the doors of perception and experience the all of it all. Be like gods.

Sitting in a Stone Boat

One day we were sitting in a stone boat,
moored by a village of fantasy
on a Welsh estuary.
The world was our untasted oyster.
We didn't know where we were going.
We were waiting for any wind to blow.
Neither of us could see
we were already sailing
on the sea of possibility.
We were unconscious of Destiny's weave.
The future was unknown
but the seeds were sown.

DAY THIRTY-FIVE

Good morning. Hoping you are *tuning in*. I'll have to do the *turning on* by myself.

Boom Shankar! Praise be to Shiva!

You've taken *dropping out* to new heights. Those Angel's Trumpets you were found underneath are also said to be the Devil's.

I hope at some level you can hear me. Because it feels kind of stupid talking to myself and telling you stories. But that's what people do, tell stories to each other. If you can hear me, make a sign, even a blink.

Everyone is missing you. The bees have left the hive and the grapes are rotting on the vine. The hens refuse to lay. You have to come back at least to make a will because there have been a few fights over who gets what. Your woodcarvings have been walking out the door. Your bonsai are walking out your garden gate.

A bikie gang have moved into your place and have been deconstructing it. They say they're looking for something that you've hidden that belongs to them. An undercover cop has been asking about you down at the local. Man, you are popular. I see why you want to stay where you are.

But what if they turn off your life-support?

Don't worry, the National Health Service will keep you in limbo until the sun dies and the rest of us are pushing up daisies.

I was joking about all the rest too.

You'll think I've lost the plot. Let me take you into the past again.

Sometimes you lost the plot and stood on your soapbox if anyone said a word like 'society', 'royalty', or even worse 'reality'! You'd really go off on that word 'reality'. It really lit your fuse. We were to deconstruct 'reality' in Goa. We were escaping from reality in one sense, escaping from what was expected of us as British citizens: that we'd get jobs, wives, settle down, watch the telly, watch the match, go to the pub, sink a few pints, throw a few arrows or play dominos, go back to the better-half, her in-doors, the missis, or try one's charms on the new lass behind the bar. We wanted to escape the sham that was Surbiton and make our own reality.

I'll read you another story about our travels:

The Journey to the East

Afoot and light-hearted I take to the open road,
Healthy and free, the world before me,
The long brown path before me leading wherever I choose.
Henceforth I ask not for good fortune, I myself am good fortune.

Song of the Open Road, Walt Whitman

Half a century ago we set off from the windy services outside Leeds, on our Journey to the East. Neither of us had thought to bring a map.

Perhaps we thought we could just say, "India", when any driver asked us where we were going and they would say, "Oh you need such and such motorway or autobahn, I'll drop you on the slip road or at the roundabout or on the corner no problem. Keep going that way, can't miss it. Follow the rising sun".

We were following in the metaphorical footprints of Alexander the Great, Marco Polo, Herman Hesse and the Beatles. It was certainly a well-trodden way. We didn't need an accompanying army, or a pack of camels, or an aeroplane. We had our thumbs for hitching rides.

I had some pills for purifying foreign waters which I thought might come in handy once we'd crossed the Channel. We had our swags, our Clint Eastwood ponchos made from Welsh wool, backpacks filled with jeans, shirts, underwear, towel, toothbrush, soap and several books, an esoteric library in fact: *Leaves of Grass* by Whitman, William Blake's collected poetry, the *Upanishads,* the *Gita, Crime and Punishment,* and a family heirloom, the Bible, which I had no intention of reading. Oh yes, mustn't forget, *The Celestial Omnibus* by E.M. Forster and the *Rubaiyat of Omar Kayam,* given to me by my father. We were natural hedonists but carried with us a fountain of gnosis in the books in our backpacks.

I had a sheath-knife that I could throw and stick into trees, a useful survival strategy I seemed sure of at the time. I had a pair of so-called desert boots and a shirt that looked like a safari jacket worn by Rudyard

Kipling. I was only lacking a topee, a monocle and cheroots. I'd bought a silver space blanket that I was assured would keep me warm in Arctic conditions. That was probably true but unfortunately one could drown in the condensation produced by body heat or wake up in saturated clothing, as I was shortly to discover. You had also packed two blue plastic sheets that could possibly make a tent.

We had passports and money we'd saved from tips earned at the hotel. I had seventy-five pounds and I think you had a bit more. I had never had such a fortune. It had been a good year. I carried my cash and travellers cheques in a money-belt around my waist, which gave me an unwelcome rash after twenty-four hours and a suspicious midriff bulge under my safari shirt.

As we set our sights on the East, I had harem dreams and thoughts of exotic conquests lying ahead down that long, winding road into my future.

Day One Has Just Begun: 10th November 1969

For some reason I wrote down in my journal what you said about this day:

I woke up and knew that I was going. Had a big breakfast: two poached eggs, baked beans.

Everyone was there. Dad was really upset.

It's really bad. You don't know what to do. Then your mother came on the bike man, that was really too much. And they took photographs, but I didn't like it.

Too much fuss all the time!

Then my father took us. It was a really bad trip. He was so proud, but it showed.

He left us at the windy services.

I wrote down what you said because I couldn't express what I felt about leaving my own parents. Perhaps I thought it unmanly to feel such emotions.

One driver who gave us a lift told us that he drove around looking for accidents. A circle of hell that Dante overlooked.

We didn't get to see any.

We were fortunate to arrive safely in Dover and find a cosy café where we listened to Bob Dylan's *Lay Lady Lay*, which conjured up erotic images in my imagination. Brother Coleman would have described them as *impure thoughts*.

We met a borstal boy who had been on parole but was heading back inside. Later, I quoted him in my account of the day:

They give you a suit which is not the real thing. I tore it to shreds. It made me feel like a spiv who thinks he's smart but isn't.

His complaints continued, punctuated with the exclamation *Bullshit!*

I'll take these biscuits. Inside I can sell biscuits two a penny, that's sixpence a packet.

If one of our House starts to hiss a screw, we all do. Can't touch us. Not if we're all together.

Half of me wants to be back, the other wants out!

His lament sounded like a dirge. He was imprisoned inside himself. When we told him of our journey to the East, he said he'd watch our ferry's departure from his cell window.

DAY THIRTY-SIX

Hello old pal. Greetings from the Village in the Rainforest and "another day in paradise" as the market-traders say. Except today there are no markets and the market-traders are in lockdown and so is everyone else. It's the virus. No international visitors thronging the streets. All gone home. The streets are empty, there's a curfew. Now the curlew patrols the main street and bandicoots fill the park, night-grubbing and dancing with quoll and echidna.

I think we are all in the Bardo, actors in an unfolding story written by Philip K Dick. It's an amalgam of ecological disaster, political blindness, social unrest and greed. Deceit poses as Truth and gets away with the mad masquerade.

Truth the Shapeshifter

I assume you are listening and one day will open your mouth and say, *No, it wasn't like that at all!* And then sit up like Lazarus back from the dead. I long to be refuted. I'm beginning to doubt the *life-narrative* that I have believed in for so long. You are the key to my doubts. You are the only one to have shared these experiences. And here you are in a coma, on life-support.

I'm still attempting to prolong my course of therapy sessions with Dr Pendrill by responding positively but not too positively to her treatment. The more stories I can tell her, the longer the stay of my execution. I have become Sheherazade! I'm sure I heard her mutter, "Sheheri" under her breath as if she could read my mind. But nothing I say or do makes her regard me any less critically. I feel I'm a specimen pinned and wriggling. Her eyes see through me. She sees my diversionary tactics, my veiled amorous flirtings. She is fixated on plumbing the depths of my memory and finding ways to rework my pathological life-narrative into a more healing one.

One night I dreamed of her. She was about five years old and so was I. We were running down a street and jumping the gaps between the paving stones. It was a matter of life or death, I remember, but we were laughing uncontrollably.

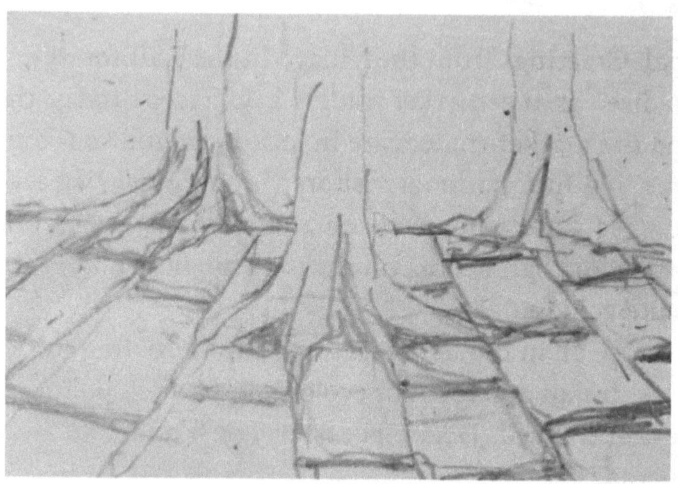

Space to grow

When I told her of the dream, she told me I have to examine the gaps in my narrative, the *lacunae*. The paving stones are the stories we tell ourselves to maintain the illusion of our existence. The gaps are the things we skate over, deny, repress, the dark side of the moon. She said these gaps have to be acknowledged to let the light in like the spaces between words.

Shit Man! She wanted me to face my demons. She had been reading my black book and filling it with yellow memo slips. She said, "We've heard a lot about your fabled Journey to the East, but nowhere have you ever said why you made the journey. And I don't want to hear those tired old New Age tropes of spiritual quests, seeking yourself et cetera".

Her fingers tracing imaginary inverted commas in the air she quoted remorselessly from my journal, making me cringe:

I'm 20 miles down the coast from Vasco, living in Consaulim on the shores of the Milky Way.

Dr Pendrill's owlish eyes blinked even wider, making me feel like a ten-year-old whose address invariably included Earth, Solar System, Galaxy, Universe, Multi-verse *ad infinitum*.

I see my journey now as a spiritual odyssey, my travels thro' Europe and Asia bringing me ever-nearer to the Self—always so close yet so distant, obscured by emotions, fears, desires, all the composites of our earthbound natures.

I see the poverty of my mind. The trip is like a book of which I only know a hundred words. Not the word. I must learn to read for this book is the Tree of Life. In its pages is the Self. All the roads of the Universe lead there.

Dr Pendrill drew final quotation marks with a flourish in the air and commented, "Very nice. Your Hindu period. I can hear George Harrison singing, *Hari Krishna, My Sweet Lord*".

She raised her eyes.

I just had to laugh at both her rather lacerating wit and my pompous juvenile posturings. She then tilted back her head and appraised me with her magnified blue-steel eyes.

So why did you go East?

I couldn't answer her, because I didn't know.

I like to imagine that one day in Portmeirion we sat ourselves down on the stone boat moored in perpetuity at the wharf and made that momentous decision, spelling out its rational underpinnings. As far as I can recall you said you wanted to hitch-hike to New Zealand and find the granddaughter of our benefactor, the architect of Portmeirion. You said you were in love with her. I didn't do a reality check and ask if the feeling was reciprocated or the family would take a waiter from Wales to its bosom. Instead I said, *Let's go.* Like the destination was down the A5. I had no idea what we would do when we came to the watery bits that lay between us and our goal. Face that obstacle when we came to it.

We never even looked at a map.

I did imagine the journey's end and the object of your adoration either rushing into your open arms or staring at you blankly as if you were an unwelcome figment of her imagination. I had no idea what I'd do in either case. What on earth was I thinking? We didn't share this romantic mission statement with anyone else, perhaps feeling it wouldn't stand up to too much scrutiny.

At an interview with the *Yorkshire Post* we claimed that we were off to New Guinea to look for gold and posed for a photograph like Victorian adventurers looking expectantly into the distance for the Source of the

Nile. I think I was wearing a safari suit and you were wearing that Clint Eastwood poncho. You just needed that dangling cheroot.

One old friend believed we were going to Borneo to live amongst the head-hunters. Another thought we went in search of the Shiva lingam in some Himalayan cavern. No doubt we fed the rumour mill over pints of bitter at the Deer Park.

When pressed by my parents for such trivial details as what we'd do when our limited funds ran out, I said optimistically something would turn up. We'd find work. We weren't work-shy, not us. I didn't suggest that we'd smuggle drugs or that being an opportunist, you'd probably sell my body, which you actually did attempt to in Persia to those unsavoury drunken companions of yours the night you karmically contracted Hep B.

Anyway, we expected that the natives of our former colonies would be delighted to offer employment to such highly personable young Englishmen who happened to be temporarily down-on-their-uppers.

So why did I decide to go East? Was I playing Sancho Panza to your Don Quixote?

Was I humouring you as one would a lunatic?

Had I nothing better to do at the time?

DAY THIRTY-SEVEN

Wakey, wakey! I've made you some porridge. You know how you love it. Honey too! Stop malingering. This is getting beyond a joke. I'm short of inspirational sayings. Here's one:

What is in the way is the way! Like your carvings man. You are always seeking to reveal your vision by taking away the unnecessary. That is the way, the chisel and knife. If you are lost in a jungle, your machete will reveal a pathway. Don't look back!

The wounded healer self-healing

On the subject of looks, my word, you haven't changed a bit. You must be halfway to Arcturus. Maybe the Bardo is that black hole at the centre of our spiral galaxy and you are heading into the Singularity. But enough speculation.

Remember the story I told you about meeting the borstal boy who said he'd watch our ferry's departure from the window of his cell. Well, at the time we had no idea how quickly our travel itinerary was to become problematic. The gods laugh when they hear humankind making plans.

Mushroom

Allons! Whoever you are, come travel with me.
To know the universe itself as a road, as many roads,
as roads for travelling souls.

Song of the Open Road by Walt Whitman

It was the morning of the second day on our *Journey to the East.*

Mushroom. You must remember Mushroom, California girl.

We met her at 3.40 am on Tuesday the eleventh of November 1969. I made a note of it in my journal, in the days before, as I wrote, *'days burst their seams'* and we were lost in time.

We were fellow passengers on the Channel ferry. It was thirty minutes before disembarking in Zeebrugge. Mushroom appeared like a forest creature, a dumpy little elf with a springy mop of curly hair. She radiated a zany 'otherness'. I thought she might have *biddies.* I was ashamed of myself for my bourgeois reaction. I didn't know it was a "bourgeois reaction" then.

Here is how you described her:

I really began to like her. She had such a strange body. Her trousers were five times too big. They used to crinkle down her leg. Crazy boots. Podgy arms. You couldn't help love her.

When you told her of our plans to hitch-hike to India, she got very excited. She was really pleased when you invited her to join us. *"Three won't be a problem"*, you said. I had reservations. Our plans already seemed jeopardised and it was only the second day of our trip. Logistically three people and their packs and sleeping swags took up quite a lot of room. Who would be bothered to stop? But I went along with you, though later you admitted having doubts too.

Yes, I definitely was playing Sancho Panza to your Don Quixote but didn't know it at the time. We were acting out some unconscious conditioning, as knights bound by the code of chivalry to offer protection to young maidens alone in the wild world. Would we have been so noble if the young woman had come from Slough and been unattractive? Were we aroused by the very notion of *"California girl"* ranking alongside *"Swedish girl"* as emissaries of Free Love, or rampant promiscuity, depending on your point of view? We had no idea. When Free Love kissed our lips, we never even knew it.

In Zeebrugge you fell asleep by the road and Mushroom and I went looking for breakfast. I noted in the journal that *I already fancied her and had conquered my aversion to biddies.* Later that day *we walked for miles and then went to sleep by a green powerhouse. Mushroom had my space blanket and we had those stupid blue things and the wind got in.*

In Brussels a nun smiled at me. After a few seconds you said, "They can tell then". I had to laugh. Whenever you wanted to mock my more retrogressive attitudes you used to say, *"Once a Catholic, always a Catholic".*

On the evening of day three a Dutchman in a truck gave us coffee and cola before sending us out into sheeting rain. We tried sleeping under his vehicle but were flooded out and *blown to an old barn, near a tank's turret, haunting a grey church. In the old barn we lay together for warmth. Mushroom lay your hand over her breast and in the morning, she turned to me.*

So it is written in my journal. It looks like a fairy tale. Did I actually see her put your hand on her breast or did it just sound good in my journal? Was I already constructing a fictional narrative?

Day Four: Mainz at 1.05 pm we were only 150 yards from the old barn, standing on the approach to the autobahn for Strasbourg. India looked a very long way away.

Why were we going to Strasbourg? That's what I was asking myself. It wasn't on the way to India. It was a detour. It was just so you could meet another girl, Francoise, a waitress you'd had a fling with back in Wales. I came self-righteously to the conclusion that you should hitch by yourself to Strasbourg and Mushroom and I would meet you there. Quite possibly I just wanted Mushroom to myself and felt relief when you actually got a lift.

The pleasure was short-lived. For some reason I consciously expurgated the narrative in my journal, leaving out moments of fright and sexual revelation. Mushroom and I were picked up by a van carrying Turkish guest-workers. She was squashed between two men in the front and I was squashed in the back with the others. I could not understand what they all were saying but it felt like they all lusted after Mushroom and were plotting her rape. They kept looking at me and laughing. My hand crept slowly down into my bag till it grasped my 'commando knife', actually just a boy-scout sheath-knife. I was ready to fight the Crusades all over again. Fortunately, it was all in my head and the van driver courteously let us off at the edge of woodland, where his road diverged from ours.

I recorded in my journal: *Mushroom and I slept in a wood, heaping leaves for a bed as though it were May and not November. In gay abandon we supped the last of my whisky and made love and then made sleep.*

Fifty years' later I ask myself who was I writing for? Why had I glossed over reality? Was it *too much to process* as people say these days? Or was it the case that I was writing a coded message for this future self to crack? I remember that we lay on the bed of leaves and she confided in me something that haunted her. Back in California one night she had taken magic mushrooms and during the trip had suffered a miscarriage. She buried the foetus in woods under the light of the moon. It is likely that this confession put a damper on my passion, reminding me of the consequences of momentary acts of pleasure outside of holy matrimony. That and my first contact with menstrual blood.

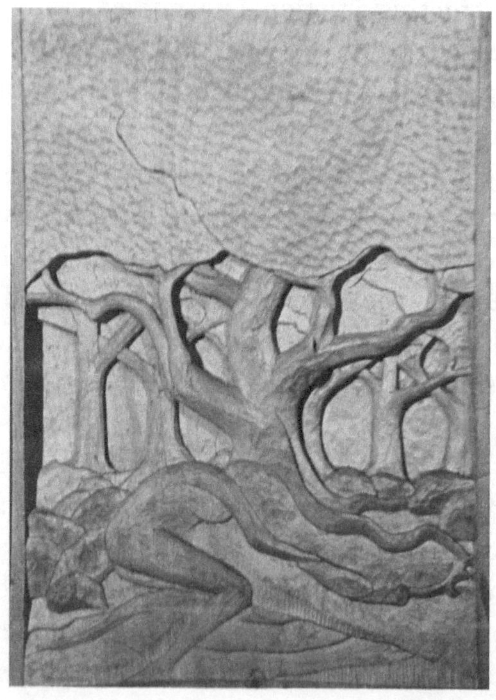

The experience was so organic it never made it into the journal. I never thought till now that Mushroom had trusted me so much that she could tell me her dark secret. I had turned the narrative into one of sexual conquest, even if it was entirely imaginary.

The following day we reached Strasbourg and I was non-plussed when Mushroom disappeared with an athletic looking Senegalese man. You also seemed non-plussed to discover that Francoise had *moved on* as we say these days and hadn't greeted you as a welcome past lover. Ha-ha! Karma, I thought to myself.

My journal entered fairy tale mode:

As night drew on and promised to be chill, they entered a tavern, there to pass the evening. And a good man (for this is how he described himself) called Bernard bought them cognac and several glasses of Bavarian beer. But it was his father's money that paid the bill.

He took them to a dancing house, but didn't dance, rather he drank more than his measure and wanted Mushroom for himself. He took them back to his home, which was in a cellar. He offered Mushroom 50 marks to do a striptease and wanted her to sleep in his bedroom.

He was so angry when she refused, he shredded his cigarettes and stuffed them in a milk bottle. He threw his arms about and made terrible threats.

We had to leave the cellar and find a place to sleep in a thicket by the autobahn.

Mushroom said these words to me:

It doesn't often happen. It is a coincidence that the two of us met. We correspond. I knew when you kissed me. I felt a power come into me and it gave me a strength knowing you felt the same way.

Now I don't know if she said those words to you and not me and I entered them in my journal after you recalled them.

That night I was non-plussed once more. We all huddled together in the thicket, but she made love to you. I lay there listening, pretending to be asleep. In the morning she said that three was a bummer for getting rides and she was leaving us and going to Paris.

She left, mounting the rise to the autobahn, bowed under her pack. At the top she turned and waved.

Now she is alone on the road and her lovers in the shadows wait.

You said later how you really loved her and wrote these words in my journal:

Only from apart can I see
I looked for silver in mountains of gold.

Dear Mushroom, fifty years in the future my tears flow in your memory.

A Night in the Black Forest

If you can't face the trolls and goblins
don't go in the forest.

That day after Mushroom left, we made little progress.

It was raining, cold November rain.

We had taken shelter in a drain that before long spat us out into a deluge and we huddled beneath those ridiculous blue plastic sheets. Later I wrote:

The call of the wood sirens
sang us to
sleeping
waking dreams of red eye and troll-
bonecold dreams
singing to us
a song of warm
nakedness
bonecold
cast a spell these young trees
fighting for light

The cold freezes the sap
this cold
comatose warmth
is bloodcold

We always maintained that it had been so tempting to fall asleep, it was a wonder that we came to our senses and got up, moved about to bring life back into saturated and chilled bodies. Like Odysseus we escaped from the siren's song. And here I am again, trying to wake you up.

DAY THIRTY-EIGHT

Greetings from Oz, old friend. Today I see that people have left flowers in your room like offerings with the promise of Spring. You remind me of Osiris in an open sarcophagus. The God of Regeneration lying like a seed in the womb of the earth.

A treescape
taking the eye into infinity
like a mandala.
You are the Mental Traveller
recording
a stereoscopic vision
on a single plane
a tale told in knots and rings
and written in the grain.

It's 2020 A.D, Annus horribilis or Annus mirabilis? Herewith some news to cheer you up:

Fewer cars, fewer trucks, less exhaust gases,
no belching smokestacks
and in the air, less air-traffic.
Clear skies everywhere from Tierra del Fuego to Alaska,
from Bradford to Beijing, Capetown to Cairo.

While the human animal is in quarantine,
around the world animals roam free.
Big cats take long naps on South African highways.
In Oz kangaroos and koalas come to town
and gangs of bush turkeys take over deserted tourist traps.

Down Indian streets
ponderous elephants sway.
Coyotes prowl the Golden Gate Bridge
and along the shore of San Francisco Bay.

Pumas roam the streets of Santiago.
Goats eat from people's gardens
in locked-down Llandudno.

Peacocks in Mumbai
let out haunted shrieks and wails,
spread their wondrous tails,
standing on the tops of cars,
their roofs and bonnets,
depositing guano.

Meanwhile the human animal
seeks salvation in song:
In the Vale of Glamorgan
residents of a street sing *Amazing Grace*
from their doorways.
And in Sienna, Italians lean from their windows
singing *Canto della Verbena* and *While Sienna sleeps,*
with municipal pride.
Residents chant in China *Keep it up Wuhan!*
and sing patriotic songs with fervour.

Around the world streets echo
to the sound of flute, clarinet or saxophone,
guitar, banjo, balalaika, fiddle, shamisen and sitar,
the beating of djembe, bodhran, snare and bongo.

Musicians join with each other,
reaching out in a time of contagion
from their isolation.

Hope this news reaches you wherever you are voyaging beyond the Solar System. And now for our recurring feature, a reading from *The Other Shore.*

The Friend

The Tibetan Book of the Dead suggests that we never see the world, only our projections that we put upon it. That's probably true, we possibly never see other people except through the same projections: Maya, the veil of Illusion.

Dr Pendrill suggested I examine the ways I have located you in my life-narrative to uncover my underlying projections. She believes the exercise will be therapeutic. I suspect that she is getting some vicarious or even voyeuristic pleasure from reading my true confessions.

Once a Catholic, always a Catholic, I can hear you say in my ear.

Looking back from fifty years' distance, I can say that I recognised an antinomian presence in you, even if I didn't have the words to express it. I knew then that you weren't normal. When you said to me once, "Fuck Dada!", I knew you were someone who had opinions about things. I admired you because I didn't have an opinion about anything, and I was in a world that demanded you had opinions about everything. I didn't tell you that I had never heard of Dada.

You became a role-model. I was your apprentice. I even changed the way I looked and sported a feathered hat and fur cloak and a pair of beetle-crushers on my feet. As common ground we shared a love of the *open road* and a longing to be *on the road again.* On the road after an extended time of waiting for a lift, say half a day, we formulated magical spells to make drivers stop. We would find a small white stone and when no cars were in sight cast it carefully onto the road. We believed that the first car whose tyres touched it would stop and provide us with a lift.

If this eventuality seemed far off, you sat by the road and with five stones you played jacks, tossing them in the air from the back of your hand and attempting to catch them in your palm and *vice versa*. You had plenty of time to practice and work on your manual dexterity. You had hitch-hiked to Sweden and south to Italy. I regarded you as an expert on the art of hitch-hiking, despite the tale of you walking through a town at night, following detour signs that after hours lead you back to the place you had started from.

Now I hear T.S. Eliot in my ears, his lines about the end of all our exploring being to arrive back where we started from and know the place for the first time.

This doesn't happen once, but in ever-repeating loops the older we get.

Not long after we had met, I must have discovered Han-shan. For some reason, I associated myself with this Tang Dynasty poet, a scholar who had tired of the city and lived as a hermit on Cold Mountain and I recognised in you, Shih-Te, his companion. Han-shan would visit the temple of Guoqing and get food scraps from Shih-Te who worked in the kitchens. These days you can Google and find pictures of the pair showing Shi-Te holding his broom to sweep out the cobwebs in our minds and Han-shan holding an empty scroll.

They would run laughing everywhere, sometimes hand in hand. Han-shan wore bark clothes. Their behaviour shocked the more conservative monks. They were the very Tao itself, the spirit of Chan. That's you! In my mind I see you standing by the sea like an Immortal, raking seaweed, now amongst your bees and growing things as the nurturing gardener, in dark winter, as the sculptor, bringing out the spirit in a block of wood with knife and chisel, ever-busy in the kitchen like Shi-Te, baking bread or stirring porridge.

I see the faces of sages in the mists, the spirits of Cold Mountain hermits.

I once read a poem attributed to Shih-Te in which he called Han-shan his only friend. They would chew magic mushrooms beneath ancient pines and chat of past and present times.

Now fifty years later I can see why I made these associations linking us with a pair of Holy Fools. We were acting out these ancient role models when we took a vow of silence that day and got fired from the restaurant in Newquay, where it seemed we eternally washed and dried dishes, pans, saucepans, cups, saucers, bowls, cutlery and peeled a mountain of potatoes that returned magically each day. We could have been in Hades with Sisyphus and Tantalus.

I have always thought of you as shamanic. I called you Shaman in a story. Your actual surname is an anagram of shaman. A fact we never realised for decades. Your connection with wood is spelled out in your name Ashman, Man of the Ash tree: a case of nominative determinism for sure.

As kundalini rises from the ground up
Illumination comes with a bolt of
lightning and a thunderclap.

You told me that the Ash is unusual in that it will always burn, even if it is green. It is always ready to let go. Like you, generous to a fault. The easiest touch on the west coast. You can't die man. You'll leave a host of guilty people wishing they'd paid you back before you left this world. I'm feeling guilty too, because I've never been able to thank you enough for just being you.

You let a block of wood speak to you.
She sings
and reveals her sylvan heart
the forest, the wood within
held in the grain of time.

Once in Goa when you were sitting in the hospital garden, you were suddenly bathed in light reflected from the pond. I wrote in my journal:

There was a redness that emanated
about his head
& emerald & turquoise
& all shades of green
clothed his body
radiant all about.

You looked like a bodhisattva.

And then there's William Blake. I was sure you were his reincarnation. You have a way of seeing things in common, like seeing the spaces around things, seeing the world in a grain of sand and holding infinity in the palm of your hand. You introduced me to his art and poetry in our shack by the beach in Goa and the pair of us have been living out his Satanic Proverbs ever since. When we drink together there comes a time when one of us says, *Too much, or not enough.* Inevitably we reply *well go on then* as the other has to fetch another bottle.

Once upon a time as you and I were travelling through the Khyber Pass you said, *Hey man, why is your head always in a book? This is the bloody Khyber Pass. You might never see it again.* I glanced at the harsh landscape, oblivious to the ghosts of Alexander's men, or those of the British soldiers who had met their end there. I continued reading *Crime and Punishment.*

Now from half a century into the future, I can see that our friendship has its depths in the ancient past, allowing us to stay filled with wonder as the beyond continues to unfold. My Cold Mountain is a tropical rainforest and the sacred language of its people. Their stories, reaching back millennia, have become my track, my Tao, my way. I have often imagined you on the other side of the world on your Cold Mountain, listening to the language of the bees, chisel running with the grain in your workshop, drinking the kind of grain found in a whisky glass whilst staggering around your kitchen extracting crumpets from the oven, the cat from the cupboard, the honey from the honeycomb.

Hard to think of you alone, without your lover, the mother of your boys.

Over the years you
grew together
found a haven
and standing side by side
in wind, snow and hail
roots and branches intertwined
you reached for sun and sky
and with your roots entangling
supped from waters underground.

DAY THIRTY-NINE

Downunder calling. Are you receiving me? Anyone out there? Just in case you can hear me, I'll carry on calmly.

I wrote these poems when I was thinking about you. My projections, as Dr Pendrill would say:

Dionysia

Your trees dance a wild bacchanalia

I think of you as ancient gods
of fertility, rebirth and resurrection
of vegetation and regeneration
of license and intoxication.

Visitors to your house
enter at their own risk
into a state
of permanent Dionysia.

From your honey you make golden mead.
Too much and all suffer amnesia.
You trample grapes you have grown
turn their juice into wine
in the never-ending quest
for *veritas* for truth
but strewth! the company you keep
often ends in chaos and disorder
and
the morning after
everyone is under the weather.

You are like Bacchus
the god of wine and ecstasy.
The god who likes to party
likes to dance.

You never sit down.
Your trees dance a wild bacchanalia.

Your guests fall asleep on the couch,
under the table
or stagger home in a trance
if they are able.

I know you can't bear that habit I have of finishing your sentences if you should pause for a moment in their flow. You don't like me presuming what you are going to say. The following poems should really annoy you. I'm writing as if I am you.

Four Elements Meditations

I am the line that creates a wall or a tree
or any particularity.
I am the space that embraces
vision like a glove fits the hand
or a ring on a finger.

Tumbled by the warm waves
onto the Other Shore
fringed by waving palms
or stepping into the cold Atlantic
over sea-slimed rocks
and raking up seaweed on the seashore
I the naked Gardener living
with the earth in all its seasons

have filled the walled garden
with my roots
year after year
and here I bloom
with the blossom of apple and pear
cherry and nectarine.

My bounty
scents the air
and feeds
a multitude of visitors
not just the butterflies
and bees.

Naked, so the body
can feel the earth, the air, the sun
the heat of autumn bonfires
or standing like a tree in the rain,
the falling snow
a blanket on my head and shoulders
initiated by the elements.

The wind and I converse
You can hear it coming from miles away
It's saying something
coming in the bedroom
and caressing me
then going back out the window.

I feel like a tree with trembling leaves
singing shush.

Wood

This is not a tree
It is me

I think of trees as me
sometimes sociable with others in a wood
or lonely, solitary
dancing in my own moonlight.

Breathe

Storm clouds seep sepia in the heavens
bearing raindrops sung up by the trees
who stand in rainbow light,
their boughs and branches
at one with the sun and the sky,
their exhalations the breath of life.
Their shadows slipping into the waters
like more spilled ink.
The sun's reflection shivers in the ripples.

DAY FORTY

Wake up! Wake up!

This is your wake-up call from my veranda. Another beautiful day in paradise. The birds are singing its praises, except for the white cockatoo who's obviously got out the wrong side of her nest. Welcome to the land of Oz.

Last time I spoke to you I tried to tell you what you mean to me. Now I'm going to tell you what Dr Pendrill might make of it all. My own fears really, my own projections.

Called to Account

Dr Pendrill's closing remarks usually start with her linking her fingers together portentously and announcing that it's time to recapitulate what we've discussed that session. Her air of finality, of saving a file and shutting down an application, made me feel the urge to capitulate once and for all.

A gecko tutt-tutted disapprovingly from the ceiling.

She picked up my black book. I felt like a bug caught in a web and paralysed by the poison of the spider. I listened mutely. "You have carried this journal for fifty years. What is its meaning for you? You maintain it represents something beyond itself, some essential meaning behind everything that has been waiting decades for you to grasp. I want you to consider its implications for you. It's time to search deeper inside yourself for the real answers".

I attempted to protest otherwise but only a strangled sound came from my mouth. With a far-sighted look in her eyes, Dr Pendrill carried on writing her session notes, but I could swear an ironic smile kept returning to her face. She placed the end of the pen between her lips and gently began to twist it. I took that as my cue to leave. As I walked away, I imagined her incisive voice cutting through my posturings:

"Is this not some juvenile pretension? You see your travels as an Odyssey and yourself as Odysseus. Do you not think you are being a trifle melodramatic, turning your hippy adventure into some kind of epic? Let's begin with the virtual hero worship of your travelling companion who seems to have led you along the antinomian path by your nose. Like Fox leading Pinocchio astray.

You identify yourself and your friend with Tang Dynasty poets, with Sufi mystics, Rumi and Shams. You believe your friend to be a reincarnation of William Blake. You think of yourselves as immortals. These identifications could be classified as totally delusional. Are you a pair of hedonists seeking pleasure and escape from social responsibilities?

So far it appears to me that your ego is somewhat hyper-inflated, full of grandiose pretensions. You have a high opinion of yourself and look down on the 'common people', the hoi polloi. This leads you to pretend to yourself that your companion is a mythical being who has shared many lifetimes with you. I detect a lurking messiah complex.

Who do you remind me of now?
(Image: Stephens Orr)

By identifying with these Holy Fools, you think you are a cut above the rest of humankind and not subject to their laws and conventions. This conveniently masks the fact you are actually two dropouts from society bent on the hedonistic pursuit of pleasure, driven by an infantile sense of magical omnipotence and a belief in Fate and Destiny, dressed in Synchronicity's clothes. It is as though you have no say in the matter, no free will. Fate becomes your way of exonerating yourself from making unsound decisions. You act as though everything is predetermined. Like a puppet, you are responding to others pulling your strings.

Your Magic Sun Kyte appears to be an attempt to write an allegory, another Pilgrim's Progress, as if truth is hiding behind mundane reality. You seek to turn the humdrum into some transcendent realm. You enter "fairy-tale mode". What did the Magic Sun Kyte really represent to you? I expect you'll say the song of innocence and experience. Freedom from the 'man-made manacles' enslaving thought.

Sounds fancy. You really mean putting off getting a proper job and facing up to reality. I begin to think reality avoidance is your default setting. You left the graveyard because it reminded you of your own mortality. You turned away from the earth to fly your magic sun kyte. You endlessly seek to escape the gravity of reality by indulging in fantasy.

The Magic Sun Kyte is a metaphor of your life experience. Illumination and clarity one moment, darkness and confusion the next. Ecstasy and her sister Despair. An attempt to reconcile your bipolarity. A journey towards psychic wholeness. A state of permanent enlightenment.

Are you dancing like Shiva Nataraj on the Demon of Ignorance or like Proust, asking where would you be without your demons? In this case your addictive behaviours.

You are the perfect example of a solipsistic narcissist. It's your last chance to dig deeper through all your Trickster evasions and your almost unique ability to switch the topic of conversation to something that seems incredibly important, but which deflects from the main issue.

You are the reincarnation of Picaro. The archetypal rogue. A vagabond. A tale-spinner. A trickster. Don't look away!

Otherwise I shall have to report you to Centrelink, as a social malcontent, a malingerer, fit for the companionship of similar souls at Sunset House, where a dedicated staff will rid you of all delusions of grandeur and speed your passing, thereby relieving the State of financial responsibility for another of its ageing population. Sunset House is full of characters you will feel at home with. There is John Lennon, Friedrich Nietzsche, two Jesuses, three Madonnas, just to name a few. Oh yes, Plato and Socrates.

Without a second thought others will dismiss your grandiose pretensions and declare that from the point of view of society you are a total failure. We have to bring you back to reality, back from the land of the lotus eaters, dry you out, eradicate those antinomian, anti-social tendencies and prepare you to become a useful member of society, willing to make sacrifices for the good of the community. That might involve a haircut, a shave and a course on dressing and personal hygiene to fit in with your fellow seniors rather than nymphs, nereids and ferals. You have to become normal or at least pass as normal. It's all up to you.

My projections about what Dr P really thinks of me have etched themselves into my consciousness, so deep that I had another dream about her. It was so real I was totally sucked in.

Black Bird Singing

As I sat in Dr Pendrill's waiting room listening to the gonging wind chimes and 'chillaxing' to the Beatles song on the radio, I wondered if the words were meant for me. If I followed her suggestions about questioning my life-narrative, I could *'learn to see'* and *'fly into the light of a dark black night'*, the dark night of my depression, illuminated by some therapeutic *inner-moon*. Had I been *'waiting for this moment to be free'*?

But I'm always reading things into things.

When I lay back on her consulting couch and out of sight of her penetrating owlish eyes, she played a video on the screen in front of me, maintaining the avian theme:

A male satin bowerbird displayed his blue-tinged trophies to interested females. The trophy collection included blue berries, quandongs, blue bottle-caps, pieces of blue plastic and a sprinkling of blue topaz crystals. The male bowerbird has violet-blue eyes and blue-black plumage. According to one theory these trophies reflect its colouring, spectral vibrations enticing the right mate.

When the video ended, there was a pregnant silence. What on earth did she expect me to say? Except I did know, so I said it. I had no option. I got a kick out of the confessional. Once a Catholic always, alas, a guilt-ridden specimens of Homo narrans, Storytelling human. Using the same jargon she'd been priming me with, I said I identified with the bowerbird. When I met with a member of the opposite sex and felt a *'glimmer'* that here was a possible *'love object'*, instead of laying out my blue trophies or flexing my muscles and beating my mighty chest, I wrote love poetry to these *'limerent entities.'*

"And what sort of cues prime that glimmering"?

Dr Pendrill swooped down on me and clutched me in her talons like a mouse or rat and shook me from side to side as if to extinguish all resistance. I couldn't stop myself from coughing it up, coming clean, spilling the beans.

I said, *I see signs, an eager look in the eye, a goddess portrait hanging on the wall, a pendant crystal nestling in a snowy bosom, a red-tailed black cockatoo feather in hennaed hair, a book of semiotics on the desk, a Beatles song.*

Dr Pendrill *happened* to be wearing a black red-tailed cockatoo feather in her hair, which had between sessions turned from steel grey to a lustrous hennaed red, a pendant blue topaz snuggled in her cleavage, the Goddess Selene looked down from her study wall and a course on semiotics by Umberto Eco lay open on her desk.

Synchronicity. Higs Boson Particles Colliding and Becoming! Entanglement! Fate! Kismet! Destiny! Will you marry me?

How could she resist me?

But Dr Pendrill was having none of it and terminated the session.

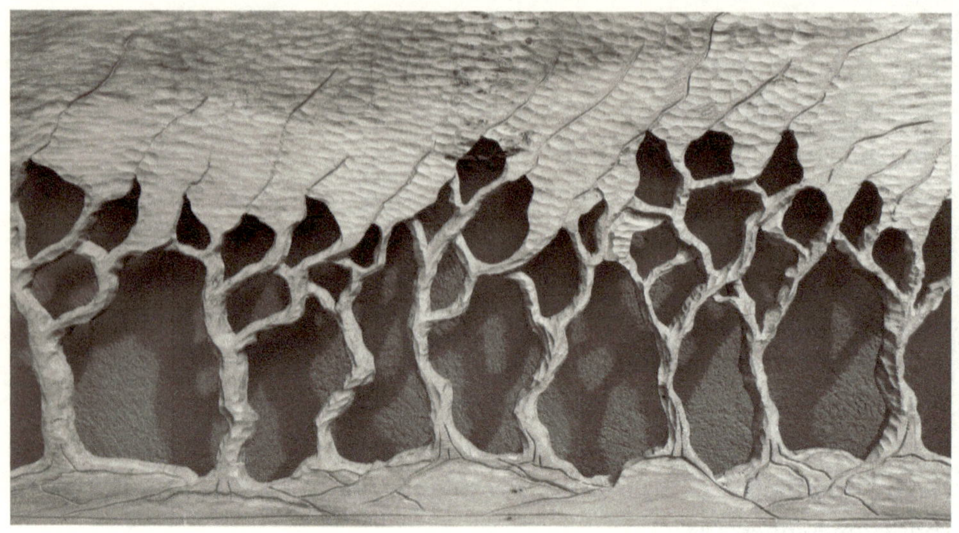

Get ready, steady, go
shake a limb, wave a bough,
rise up on your roots and do
the deadly Dryad Boogaloo.

DAY FORTY-ONE

Downunder calling Scotland. Are you receiving me? You really should make an effort. I've just had a lovely chat with your nurse. Drop dead gorgeous. A redhead of course. Her name's *Hela*, would you believe? *Goddess of the Underworld.* She has always wanted to come to Oz, so I invited her. She said she'd be on the first flight Downunder when the pandemic is over. You'd better wake up fast, man. She was glimmering all over.

Just joking! She told me your condition was unchanged. It's true, you look like you did yesterday and all the days before. You've been in the Bardo for forty-one days. I hope you can hear me. Please open your eyes and look at this mob of flying fox returning to their trees to hang upside down and dream the day away.

I was telling you about my dream. Well this is what my Dr Pendrill said about it.

Limerent Entity

"That dream you shared where I possessed all the attributes of a Limerent Entity, a possible Love Object, is obviously a case of transference. Everything you feel about another is transferred to your therapist, in this case me.

In divulging your past to me you are replicating what happens when you open up to a potential Love Object, in whom you detect a 'glimmering' potency. You confess to things you might never have told your own partner, or significant other. Let's be clear, I am not the one you are seeking".

Dr Pendrill pointed at herself, underlining the statement, "I am your therapist, or rather life-readjustment coach". As she said these words it seemed that her eyebrow twitched ironically. But I couldn't be sure. I was always misinterpreting signs given by women and had got into lots of trouble. When I looked in her eyes, I was sure that I'd looked into them a very long time ago. If only I could remember.

"It can't be a coincidence that I've found you here," I said.

"It isn't a coincidence. I am here to reflect yourself back to you."

I am sure that Dr Pendrill winked at me, but maybe it wasn't a wink, more like a predatory owl's blink, before she continued:

"We need to re-examine your river of life-narrative and discover where you've gone up the wrong creek or stagnant backwater so to speak and become alienated and addicted to alcohol and banned substances.

Having listened to you for some time now, one of the most interesting things about your case is not the confessions by which you put such store but the omissions that inevitably accompany them.

For each confession there is at least one far graver and far-reaching omission, which lingers in the background unspoken. I'm quite sure that these omissions whatever they are, are the ones you see as the most threatening.

Take the glimmers out of your eye! I am your psychotherapist not some interchangeable love-object. Now lie down on the couch and talk."

Dr Pendrill sat behind me out of sight and I lay on the couch like a pinned insect or a flayed carcass. For some reason I had turned up my trouser bottoms as if I were a beachcomber. The whiteness of the calves looked ridiculous. I couldn't let her write me off. I had to keep her interested in making a case-study of me. I was willing to sing in the spilling-the-beans sense, but first I tried out a technique I'd learned from my father who'd quote Shakespeare at the drop of a hat and make everyone forget what they were on about. I spouted T.S. Eliot.

"And I have known the eyes already," but I only got as far as "pinned and wriggling on the wall" when she cut me off curtly.

"I see you wear the bottoms of your trousers rolled and have no doubt lingered in the chambers of the sea and been wreathed with seaweed by sea-girls too. Thank you, Mr J. Alfred Prufrock, let's stick to your past identity as Sam."

Although her face was deadpan, I could detect under her words the quivering notes of suppressed laughter, almost as hidden as the omissions I myself was leaving out of the conversation. Instead of fretting about my disclosures as I would have done in the confessional, I found myself instead fascinated by the idea of a Dr Pendrill who could not only sweep her legs in a slow sensuous curve but also do so with apparent amusement at my discomfiture. I was so carried away that when she said, "I think it's time to get behind your ego's defensive wall and put you under hypnosis", I agreed.

"We have already talked over your past loves and it brings to mind a certain Don Juanism."

I told her that I'd always been a fan of Carlos Castaneda and his sorcerer Don Juan, but she cut through my evasion with her penetrating analysis, leaving me stunned.

"Do you have a mother complex? You say you are a serial monogamist. Who is the partner you are looking for in these different women who each have some Pre-Raphaelite enchantment about them? Redheads, alabaster skin? The poet Goethe formulated it, very appropriately in your case, as "seeing Helen in every woman". How many of your lovers have been mothers? Are you looking for your mother? Do you put each new lover on a pedestal? See them as a goddess or a muse and when you find that they are merely human move on in search of a new lover or rather, another mother."

I nearly choked.

"Now lie back on your couch and watch the screen." The lights went out and the screen in front of me filled with water.

"I call these waters the Storywaters. Look into the waters."

The water had suddenly turned turquoise and I was sitting by a poolside. I was thirteen years old and was a guest at a birthday party. I had always fancied the birthday girl and now I couldn't keep my eyes off her as she dived like a water nymph then lay on her back, floating on the surface, her lustrous red hair streaming around her head. But when I had a chance to talk to her, I couldn't say a word. I couldn't look her in the eye. I couldn't say her name.

She was the Myerscough girl of course. Her name was Helen!

The screen filled with water the colour of green jade. I could hear Dr Pendrill reading from my journal.

"Daisy, Rose, Tulip. Beautiful flowers."

I am by the sea on Calangute beach in Goa and someone has written the words in the sand. As I look at the words they are already being washed away. Then I see a mermaid sculpted in the sand.

"A starfish ornaments her navel, pearls are her eyes and her body is already dissolving in the reaching tide," I hear Dr Pendrill's voice.

Further along the beach I find more sand sculptures. Two women making love. Someone with no appreciation of fine art has left behind the imprint of a foot on the bottom of the one on top. The corrugations of the sand turn into an infinite orgy of people fucking beneath my feet.

And now I am sitting on the beach with you and you are studying Genesis. I see a woman coming towards us and eyeball her bright hennaed dreadlocks and the pale moon of her face. I am surprised when she sits not far from me and try not to look as she takes off her saffron robe and strides out into the sea. I watch her diving into the waves like a mermaid or a goddess. The sun makes a halo of her flaming hair. Then she turns around to come back to shore and I see her startling alabaster breasts, the red-gold of her pubes and a white dangling penis. I cannot believe my eyes. It is not Venus emerging from the waters but the child of Hermes and Aphrodite, Hermaphrodite.

I want to let you know what I am looking at, but you are immersed in the Bible. It didn't seem appropriate anyway. I suddenly felt like Benny Hill nudge-nudge-wink-winking. As the apparition comes towards me, I see that he ... she ... is looking at me and smiling, perhaps grateful that I hadn't told you to check out the view. The apparition put on the saffron robe and began walking back along the sands. I never tell you what I have seen. I couldn't put it into words without cheapening the experience, the vision. Those eyes seemed to look into my soul and laugh at my astonishment.

I hear Dr Pendrill's voice reading from the journal.

"At night we stand by the sea and see the stars, the storm-lamps of the fishermen, and listen to their joyous song for the catch is large. With nets they run from the sea to spill the silver fish onto dancing heaps."

DAY FORTY-TWO

Hey man! Wake up! There's a lot of people who love you, a growing list of lady-friends. Who are you, man? Lord Krishna himself with his cowgirls? You are surrounded by even more flowers, still in cellophane wraps in case they harbour the virus.

I've got a titillating tale for you this morning. Should bring back some memories.

A Flash of Emerald Green Satin

Dr Pendrill held my journal in her hands with yellow memo slips poking up through its pages.

I wasn't looking forward to this session. This was worse than going to confession. Dr Pendrill held the key to my fate. She seemed half-therapist, half-inquisitor. And sometimes, like now, I imagined she fancied me.

She sat me down and drew up a chair directly in front of me. I eyeballed her as discreetly as possible. Just like in the dream she'd hennaed her pixie cap of white hair. Her emerald green blouse revealed a flash of topaz pendant, nestled in alabaster cleavage and the tantalising white lace of her bra, as she sat down in the chair and teased off her high heels. I'm sure I heard a crackle of static as she crossed her stockinged legs. I didn't know where to look. I wished I could retreat onto the couch.

She must be at least my age but not one wrinkle or worry line blemished her glowing face, as if she'd discovered the secret of longevity, the fire within. She opened the journal and began to read. As she read, she swayed from side to side on her ergonomic chair by the slight pressure of her stockinged feet on the floor. I couldn't help noticing her black skirt riding up her thighs but tried to concentrate on the words she was quoting and detach myself from the sudden rising tide of my libido.

The entry Dr P read was made in Goa on the twenty third of January 1970, fifty years ago:

To the Shalimar. Today we saw a girl of sixteen or so. She was a powerful lady, each smile, eyes, perhaps not so innocent behind dark sunglasses.

Dr P noted that I had switched to your account, saying:

I watched her and she saw me looking at her legs. She thought I couldn't see her eyes.

Dr Pendrill's motion on the chair seemed to speed up and I couldn't help noticing a flash of emerald green satin between her thighs. I tried to blank my mind, I even appealed to Lord Ganesh to help me overcome obstacles to Satya, but she continued remorselessly:

the girl leaned back, moved her body forward in the chair and her skirt rode up. She looked down and pulled it back even further. She knew what was happening. And she had frilly knickers. I'd never seen a girl so hungry man.

I glanced at a clay tablet on the wall above Dr Pendrill's head, attempting to escape from where this was going.

"Baubo will not rescue you. She is laughing at your disavowal of a primal fascination."

Dr Pendrill stopped her chair's motion and gazed at me questioningly, her blue-grey eyes seeing deep into my soul. I'm sure my face was red with embarrassment. I looked back steadily into her eyes hoping they wouldn't look down at the tell in my trousers.

"You saw this girl too, so how is it that you use your friend's words and not your own? Is it that you want to distance yourself from this erotic encounter and not admit to sharing the same fascination: scopophilia, perhaps, or fetishisation of underwear? Is this a way of smuggling into your journal things you might be ashamed to have to account for, by using your friend as mouthpiece?"

I was rendered mute; my increasingly visible physiological stress proved her point. She started to read another entry, quoting what you had said about an experience with a girlfriend called Laurel, before our travels to India:

We were running so fast downhill to a ravine and climbing up. And the top was smooth with little pools and the stars shone there. Lying and singing and kissing. And I've never seen a girl get so drunk on half a cider. We went for a drink and on the way back she threw back her head and was laughing. That was the night I smashed the car — but she was saying Fuck! Fuck! Fuck! All the time.

Dr P paused to prompt me again, "Are you using your friend's reminiscences to make up for your own lack of sexual experience? Did you get vicarious pleasure from re-telling his romantic exploits, his dreams, his expletory freedom?"

As I listened the tide of my libido retreated as fast as it had risen. What she said was true. At that time, I had considered you as some kind of sex guru and loved listening to your amatory exploits, which decades later I learned were mainly fabricated by my own mind. Mind you, I think you enjoyed leading me up the garden path or to Ilkley Moor. I have a 'clear' memory of you telling me that once you had stolen a condom from your father's packet that you'd found in the bathroom mirror-cupboard. This you totally denied, saying that it was inconceivable that such an item would ever have been in such a place. I am learning that my 'memories' are always constructs, sometimes enshrining untruth as truth.

My journal is a case in point. It is what it doesn't say that is loaded with significance, as if I was consciously censoring myself.

Who was I writing for?

Bad language was proscribed throughout my childhood. There was a realm of the unsayable.

Who was I afraid might read the manuscript?

Looking back from fifty years in the future, I can answer the last question. Mom.

But Dr Pendrill answered the question for me. She postulated that I was a perfect example of the *Puer Aeturnus,* the Eternal Youth. I knew where she was going with this, so I tried to escape the net of her words by referring to Ovid's *Metamorphoses*. I said, "Ovid praises the child-god Iacchus for his role in the Eleusinian mysteries and calls him *Puer Aeturnus*. He was the torch-bearer, leading a riotous procession of the initiated to Eleusis, dancing to the sound of cymbals and trumpets."

Dr Pendrill was not to be distracted, "That's true, if you're quoting the textbook. The child-god is also identified with Dionysus and the god Eros. He is a god of vegetation and resurrection, a redeemer figure even." But then she cut me down to size, saying, "However, I am not referring to the *Puer Aeturnus* in that sense. I am referring to a certain type of young man who has an outstanding mother complex. And is a cheeky monkey".

"Oh really," I complained. "But I left home! I couldn't wait to get on the road."

"You were fleeing from reality and responsibility, making a break for imagined freedom, denying a sense of rootedness. Escaping from the mother figure, though she remained, forever looking over your shoulder, censoring your literary efforts. The greatest fear of such a person is of being 'pinned down', of being bound down to anything whatever, any obligation. Passing from woman to woman, always looking for the perfect mother goddess to see to all his needs and comforts. Believing that he is the bearer of a sacred truth, a kind of redeemer, a messiah even, that one day everyone will recognise. Sounds familiar?"

"What a bastard," I said, laughing hollowly.

DAY FORTY-THREE

Man! Wake up! You won't believe what we have to do these days if we want to go to Foodworks. Because of my age I'm allowed in at 7 am. On entry you have to wash your hands with antiseptic and wipe down the handle of the shopping trolley. Some people are wearing masks and look at you as if you should know better. You have to keep a metre and a half from other shoppers and stand on marked out spots when approaching checkout. Whatever you do, you mustn't cough or even worse let out a sneeze.

And there are no bog-rolls left in Australia!

Some places won't accept money anymore, only cards. One hears whispers that Big Brother is tightening his grip on the population by taking away cash from the people's pockets and making them depend on digital transactions. Freaky!

I want to tell you about the effect your art is having on my psyche. It's freaky too but in a good way. I've been looking at those photos of your Celtic carvings. They prompted a dream last night.

The Book of Unknowing

I am in the presence of a book that lies open on an altar in some etheric plane. It seems to be illuminated from within and radiates the light of infinite understanding.

It emanates the numinous like the occult Akashic record of the imaginative Theosophists.

It is written in another language, which with mounting excitement I find myself reading.

Each page is like a palimpsest with different strata of sense and meaning glimpsed simultaneously.

The text is at one with its visual representation, an erotic coupling of sound and vision.

As I hear myself reading the words, the dream dissolves like salt in water, leaving me clutching my pillow and feeling a deep sense of loss, of bathos, of having been on the edge of a cosmic revelation and now wondering whether to have marmalade on toast and a cup of tea or attempt to re-enter the dream and find true wakefulness on the highest astral plane.

The toast and tea won the contest.

I'm having them now for breakfast. Wish you could join me for some mango, pawpaw, custard apple, black sapote, need I say more.

Time to take you back to *The Other Shore.*

Remember that time when we split up in Delhi?

Dr Pendrill wanted to know why we had parted. She has this knack of spotting those things I wish to skate over, sins of omission, avoidance of the truth. Reminds me of a priest in the confessional.

Little can be gleaned from my black book about my reasons for leaving you. The whole episode leaves me feeling like Judas Iscariot. No wonder I skated over it. Delhi was hot, dry and dusty and the air was tinged with tear-gas. We were staying at Mrs Colasso's guesthouse and I had the flu or something, fever, bad throat. That meant I couldn't smoke with you and your new chum Mozart. I began to look at you through the lens of sobriety and feared the worst. How could we continue on our quest together when you were off your face? I began to regard you and Mozart as bad company, lost in a cloud of ganja. I called Mozart 'Mr Too Much', because that's what he kept saying every other minute.

On January the first I wrote, *Everyone is mad. Money! Money! Money! cries Mrs Colasso.*

There was a Dutch lady staying there, Tineke. Although she was old enough to be my mother, I felt attracted to her. She seemed to be on a spiritual quest too, a path of understanding. I confessed to her that I was confused and had no idea which way to go. I threw the I Ching coins and she read the oracle. Chien/Obstruction. The south-west furthers. The north-east does not further. It required me to persevere when apparently one must do something that leads away from the goal. An obstruction that lasts for a time is good for self-development.

I threw the coins again.

What a coincidence! It told me to Cross the Great Water. That had been our original plan.

Go to Bombay, find a ship to stowaway on and sail into the blue yonder.

The reading reconfirmed my resolve. I should have realised that Goa was in the south-west and gone with the flow but it's easy with hindsight to see where we go wrong.

You and Mozart wanted to go to Goa and smoke yourselves silly. But we all had to get to Bombay first, so we needed railway tickets. We scored some counterfeit student cards to get railway concessions and went to book our tickets. The man in the booking office looked at our student cards and picked up his phone.

That's how we ended up being interrogated by a railway police officer. He scrutinised our student cards and found it odd that our identity numbers ran consecutively. You claimed it was just a coincidence. He replied that it certainly was. In fact, he thought it highly suspicious given that, although you and I were at the same college in Leeds, Yorkshire, England, our companion was allegedly attending an art school in Stuttgart, Germany. He had reason to suspect that our cards were counterfeit and that we could be prosecuted for attempting to defraud the Railway.

I saw that he had a point, but you two madmen persisted in protesting your innocence. Rather than go down with the pair of you, I decided to come clean, admit the truth and not exasperate the police officer into doing something we'd all regret. As an immediate consequence the police officer handed me back my student card, allowing me to get a student concession. He retained the other two student cards and made you pay full price for your tickets to Bombay before sending you on your way with a stiff warning not to transgress again.

In your eyes I could see I had betrayed you. I felt like a dirty rat. I heard your words in my head, *Once a Catholic, always a Catholic.* Goody-goody pure boy! I caught the next train to Agra. I thought I'd never see you again.

But we weren't yet done. To our mutual surprise we met in Agra and I caught the same train as you and Mozart, bound for Bombay. But on the way to Bombay, I abandoned you again. It was the day you began coming down with hepatitis and had a fever. I left the train to go looking for the Buddha at the Ajanta caves. The only message the Buddha had for me was an empty hand.

Half a century later I see that the Buddha told me everything I need to know.

When I reached Bombay my dreams of stowing away and Crossing the Great Water evaporated, and I ended up catching a boat to Goa in the rather foolish hope that I could find you.

I just went with the flow and followed the *flower people*, disembarking in Panjim and crossing the Mandovi in a dug-out canoe to catch a motorbike ride to Calangute. Three days later I saw you in a chai shop. You didn't look very well.

I'm looking at a photo you took of me and one of your fellow patients.

Garden of Dreams

We had ended up in Goa in Panjim hospital with you recovering from yellow jaundice. Bung was a patient there. He had high blood pressure. A vein had burst in his forehead years before. He'd been paralysed in his legs and arms. Nobody would tell him what was wrong but warned him that if he got too excited it would happen again and kill him. He told us that as a consequence he had worked for fifteen years in an office quietly doing the same thing every day and saving for the biggest motorcycle in the world.

I can't wait to say, "Come and have a look at it. Then I'll be off, full throttle. I'm not stopping till my gas runs out".

Maybe we both said, *"Far out, man!"* Most things were *far out* in those days.

Bung also described where he found bedded bliss for 50 rupees a night. We rashly encouraged him in his death-defying existential quest for excitement.

We were sitting in the hospital garden next to the lily pool and smoking Kashmiri in joints rolled with Chardinar or Passing Clouds. We had no idea that Bung would have a role to play in our fate. Nor did Bung know that he would become a character in a story written half a century later. He was simply a patient at the hospital where you were being treated for Hepatitis B.

When I first visited, you said you were woken at six for blood samples, gallons and gallons and then at seven, dark urine specimens were taken. Your bed was crawling with bed bugs, who shared what blood you had left. However, you had met a delightful night nurse. I didn't show much sympathy.

I worked out that you'd caught hepatitis in Iran, on the night you got drunk on vodka and were going to sell me to your drinking companions. Instant karma? Poetic Justice? I ask myself snidely. Your skin was yellow, but I knew you were on the way to recovery. In my memory I visited you every day, but according to my journal my visits were sporadic, though consciousness-changing. I did not complain that I had spent a night in the park and been eaten alive by mosquitos just so I could pay a visit. I didn't want to bring you down. Actually, I tell a lie. I probably did grumble. I just edited it out of my journal's account so I could appear as Sam, the good Samaritan.

Some details come from the journal, but there were some things I didn't record. You asked me to find the longest book I could, and I found *Mardi* by Melville. There was a speech somewhere in it that dispelled all fear of death. I recommend it to anyone who is death phobic, but I can't remember the page. Better get reading.

Under the palm trees on a bench by the lily-pond, we sat and smoked hashish all day in the hospital garden. Nobody seemed to mind. Hospital life went on around the periphery, but we were out of it. We'd learned how to say *Boom Shankar* and offer smoky libations heavenwards. We were at the still-point of the turning universe with enough hashish in our lungs to maintain the illusion.

Plop! Plop! Plop!

Wow, man, did you see that?

A frog appeared to leap across the pond by jumping on water. This became a *cosmic event*, although on closer examination we could plainly see lily-pads just beneath the surface.

Once I looked at you and saw you illumined by light reflected from the pond. A red halo emanated around your head and emerald and turquoise and all shades of green clothed your body. You began recalling the event of your own birth complete with lucky caul and I imagined sitting there forever as you described all the happenings of your life. I realised that, once started, you could never catch up with the present, because the present doesn't keep still.

On your last morning at the hospital we duly celebrated with Bung and Scrounger. Bung was a glucose fiend and was always after your allowance. Scrounger was one too. He got jealous of Bung and traded bananas for your stash. *Boom Shankar!* we proclaimed, taking gulps from the chillum in turn and watching smoke drift heavenwards.

We left Bung behind, never expecting him to track us down. It's not as if we knew where we were going. We were drawn south and ended up at a shack by the railway line at Consaulim, on the northern end of Colva beach, Goa. We intended to stay there while you recuperated.

DAY FORTY-FOUR

Good morning my dear listener. Well I hope you are listening. This is what it's all about. Bringing you back! Mind you, the world you'll come back to is like a ghost world. Just like your Bardo. In town all the souvenir merchandise lies behind locked doors waiting maybe never to be sold: a thousand and one didgeridoos, bikinis made from roo fur, purses made from the males' scrotums, furry little kangas, koalas and stuffed crocodiles galore. The streets are still empty, shops all closed, no market, no pub, no people. Ghost town. I wander the streets and it feels uncanny. Like I'm the only one alive. Me and my shadow. And the birds rejoicing.

Looking into your art I reckon I'm falling into your Bardo, shadow dancing

It's About Letting Go

"It's about letting go," you said. I have to agree.

I wonder why Consaulim is the place my mind is drawn back to like no other. The shack by the railway track had been our haven for what seemed an eternity. But we knew we had to move on. We left our packed bags with Bung and went to say good-bye to the beach and the people of the sea. I must've had some presentiment because I took with me my passport and remaining fifty dollars in travellers cheques. I felt a bit guilty about not trusting Bung. He'd turned up the night before. How he'd found us I've no idea.

He'd brought a tola of *Manali* and we'd spent the night in hash heaven, lying on the cow-dung floor of our hovel. I wished that I could be as trusting as you, for without a trace of irony you had told Bung to make himself at home. In fact, you said *Help yourself. We won't lock up.* Bung wobbled his head in agreement as if his head was on a spring. We knew he was catching the four o'clock bus to Vasco and didn't want to cast him out. I was supposed to be an enlightened being, beyond material needs and yet I worried about things like leaving Bung behind us in the shack.

We'd hitchhiked the Old Silk Road. We'd followed the Hippy Trail. We'd gone back in time and witnessed the birth of the universe: the beach that mirrored eternity in the repeating pools left by the retreating tide, the dug-out canoes, the fishing nets, survivals of an ancient race caught in the global marketplace. This was not any beach. It was the place we'd always been searching for, Consaulim of the Soul, a goal which we'd been seeking, a haven to make some kind of sense of it all, a liminal state where we could not hear the Voice of the Machine. Except of course for the railway train reconnecting us with the World of Time as it rattled by and let out a blast of steam.

It seemed for the first time in our lives that we were free. You were recovering from the Hep B and your skin was losing its yellow hue. You let your body go with the sea's ebb and flow and be tumbled up the sands like flotsam. We had left one life behind and were looking for meaning in the chaos of it all. The meanings we found were so profound they disappeared with the morning light. We had undergone a cosmic shift of paradigms.

We had not heard of Derrida, but we deconstructed everything from God to Society and the notion of Self, even Death.

We heard the sound of one hand clapping. We were Zen masters and pearls of wisdom fell from our mouths. We should've written them down because by dawn they'd vanished like a dream. You rewrote the Gospel of John, blotting out each article or preposition you thought unnecessary so as to perceive the inner meaning. You left a text that is unintelligible to others. Unfortunately, your corrections defaced my family heirloom, but I let it go. I was turning Hindu, I wanted to be a sadhu.

There were days I lost my faith and travelled by bus and boat and motorbike to Anjuna to score ourselves some *Sat Chit Ananda*, Being Awareness Bliss. I'd return and see you sitting on the window-ledge. I called you *The Celestial Tea-maker*. How could we leave this place? Here I'd been born again.

Once, from a man who looked like Bacchus, I bought a pumpkin seed of LSD, guaranteed to be as good as *California Sunshine*. As I held the orange, grainy, psycho-active seed in my palm you recited William Blake:

> *To see a World in a Grain of Sand*
> *And a Heaven in a Wild Flower,*
> *Hold Infinity in the palm of your hand*
> *And Eternity in an hour.*

As I swallowed it, I wondered if I'd come back again. Would I be the same? I remembered Alice. The first thing I saw were the spaces between the palm fronds. The horizon was clouded. I was disappointed as if I were watching a film with second-rate special effects. I didn't realize that I was *the Mental Traveller* and that *the eye altering, alters all.*

The sun slips behind the cloud and the wet sands to the north turn red and pink and cherryade and to the south emerald green. A wall of night is slipping up from behind us over the jungle.

You were sitting on the squeaking white sands reading from the Bible and I was walking at the edge of the sea as the Spirit moved over the Waters of the Deep. I stepped outside myself. Suddenly I was the Universe looking out at itself. I was the World Self. I was without limit, boundless. I was lost in wonder at the starry drift above and the tug of the wavelets around my feet.

Some boys came over and asked you what I was doing.

You said that I was walking on the sands.

They asked you what you were doing, and you replied that you were sitting, watching me walking on the sands.

To me you said, *You are seeing, man! Worlds, galaxies, atoms.*

I was thinking I'd fall through the spaces of the world like Alice. My body was vibrating like a bell. My mind was having revelations:

I am spirit in the form of man.

I am the universe looking out through my eyes.

In my ears the waves of the sea sing like a choir of angels.

Above: a heaven of stars.

Below: in purple shades the eternal shore, the silhouette of fishing boats, silver foam, silver surf.

From the jungle's edge: fires of the fisher folk, shouts and crickets talking.

I am lost in the immensity of it all, suffocating, drowning in life.

You presided over the rite of passage, smoking chillums of temple balls to keep up.

As I paddled on the edge of the sea, one side of me wanted to dive into the dark waters. The other side said, *Fuck that.* Something touched me on the ankle. It was a shock to find myself embodied. I stepped back. I had forgotten how to put on the clothes I'd shed like a chrysalis on the vocal sand. Nor could I remember the way back. You had the candle ready and led me back along the path. I saw snakes everywhere in snaking roots. Even dead leaves were living in the breeze.

Our shack was a psychedelic cavern and I found clothes that belonged to me and an identity that I had lost and found again. I looked at my photograph in the passport and saw family resemblances on my mother and father's sides, a genetic stamp going back in time like a potter's signature. I felt like an extra-terrestrial agent sent to Earth, equipped with a human body and a ready-made legend in this place we had found ourselves. We felt like castaways on the shores of the Milky Way where the waves of the sea were lapping.

And now we were saying good-bye. We were intending to leave early the following day.

We had crab curry with the fishing people. Then we stood down by the sea. It was windy and sand was dancing high over the shore on which green foam-laced waves were racing. Looking along the beach I saw nets, an anchor, fishing boats drawn up above the reach of tide. The fisher girl with the peony in her hair waved to us for the last time.

We followed the familiar track between the palms back to the shack. The door was open but there was no sign of Bung. Bung had helped himself to all your money and 190 rupees from my wallet. He had left us three rupees. The man next door said he had seen it in his face. You chased after him and told me you'd glimpsed his bus leaving. I imagined him looking back at you and wobbling his head and making that sign that means from the god in me to the god in you, *Namaste.* Bung was on his way to bedded bliss or disappearing into the horizon on the bike of his dreams. *But look he left the Manali!* You showed me and then, crumbling it in your fingers, you added it to a *Passing Cloud. It's about letting go,* you said, passing me the chillum.

Boom Shankar, I said, but I still had my remaining travellers cheques in a purse under my shirt.

DAY FORTY-FIVE

Top of the morning to you from here on the veranda. Listen to the thundering frogs. They are singing up the rain. I see your mountain of flowers is growing. I think some of them have come from your own garden. If you come back to the living, you'll have to hack your way through them. But in the meantime, let's go back to Goa.

The Day I Inherited the World

We left Consaulim the day after Bung had done a runner with all your worldly wealth. We went north to stay on Calangute beach with friends we'd made.

You had written to your parents asking for financial assistance and were waiting for money to arrive at the nearby bank in Panjim, whilst I had fifty American dollars in my hidden travellers cheques and with a bit of luck and extreme austerities could make it back to England. I had to exchange my dollars on the black-market to make sure I got the most I could, so I didn't exchange them in Panjim. I rationalised that if I stayed and shared my remaining dollars with you, I'd be a liability for you when your financial packet landed. I left you to your fate and suffered *instant karma*. Not quite instant. I reached Poona and had to accept the poor exchange rate of the bank. I scored some far-out charass and hallucinated Shiva sitting below the bridge on the riverbank. A sadhu, combing out his glossy black hair as the river flowed by.

Hitching rides on trucks that resembled mighty chariots of the gods, I reached Ahmedabad fourteen days later, suffering from food poisoning. Sitting by Lake Kankaria, recovering from an attack of diarrhoea, I watched the full moon rising until hordes of mosquitos persuaded me to find a hotel room for the night. In the city, I met two young students, brothers, who wanted me to stay with them at their parent's house. The parents made a fuss of me and gave me a bed and their only electric fan.

After a perfect night's sleep, I awoke refreshed and discovered that my dirty clothes had been washed and dried and were neatly piled beside my bed. This was better than any hotel. I was given a cup of chai and sat as guest of honour whilst the neighbours crowded into the room to meet me. I was probably the first ever Englishman to set foot in their street and the old man, the father, proudly turned on a radio, to let me hear a play being broadcast in English. I was not so interested in the play and began asking about the different gods depicted in the posters that decorated the walls: Shiva and Vishnu, Ganesh and Krishna. But then we came to a goddess that I didn't know. She was standing on a lotus leaf and showering gold coins into the waters. My bag lay on the floor directly below the poster.

"Who is she?" I asked.

"She is Lakshmi, Goddess of Fortune."

As I heard the words, I knew my stash of dollars had disappeared from my bag.

An image from the poet WH Auden came into my head, of *a stream in a limestone country*. The stream was my fortune and it had slipped out of sight down some sinkhole and now ran through caverns deep underground. I had to get up, cross the room and search my bag. My passport was there, but the purse containing my money had vanished. I turned my head to look at the old man just as words from the radio play entered my consciousness: *You have stolen my money. You have stolen my money!* As my eyes met the eyes of the old man, his eyes seemed to fill with tears, and he turned away.

I reeled back and sat down on my seat. It felt uncanny. I felt like some initiate in an ancient mystery being shown that life is the never-ending play of the gods. What on earth was I going to do? How could I ever get back home? Was I going to spoil an otherwise delightful morning and suddenly charge my hosts with theft? Could I suggest to my two friends that their father was a thief?

I suddenly thought of you. Why I wonder? I had scarcely given you a moment's consideration since I'd hit the road. But the thought of you filled me with a sense of calm and empathy. This poor family had shared their home with me. The actual amount of money I'd lost would not have paid for one night at a luxury hotel. I decided to say nothing about the theft but sat there, wondering what to do now that I was as destitute as you.

The two brothers asked me to accompany them to the temple before setting off on my journey back to England. I welcomed the suggestion. It meant I could put off dealing with the fact that I'd just become impoverished. As I made my farewells to the parents and thanked them for their hospitality, I felt an inexplicable feeling of happiness. I've since learned it's called dopamine and is the reward for random acts of kindness and empathy.

Inside the temple were two vast murals. The first depicted scenes from hell. Humans were being tortured by demons in all manner of ways. I realised that these fiendish tortures had been devised by men and that even as I was staring at the painting, the real thing was taking place somewhere in the world. This mural was reflecting reality, not some imaginary future state of being.

Predictably the next mural showed scenes from paradise. It depicted handsome men and voluptuous women enjoying a life of plenty, set to celestial music, amidst beautiful gardens with splashing streams. It reminded me of Goa. I realised that all over the world many were actually living in paradise and that the two murals depicted very real extremes of human existence.

Then my companions led me into the *sanctum sanctorum*, the holy of holies. This was a dark room with a single source of light illuminating an image of Krishna playing his flute. He was reflected to infinity by mirrors on either side. I felt I'd been admitted to the still point at the centre of the whirling universe. In the midst of dissonance, I heard harmony, in the midst of chaos, I perceived an underlying order, in the midst of darkness, I'd found light.

We left the temple and I said goodbye to my friends. They wished me luck as I walked away to find the long road back home.

I felt lucky. I'd just found two rupees in my pocket. I felt like I'd just inherited the world.

DAY FORTY-SIX

Hello it's me again. Time you said hello. I'm getting sick of the sound of my own voice!

It's all about letting go

I'm looking at one of your carvings and seeing in it the notion of surrender, of acceptance of life's process. The cleft bough still cleaves to its tree. I'm still clinging to a wobbly tooth.

Back to the day I lost my money.

The Cockroach

I must have come out of the temple with an aura around me for I was befriended by a man called Ramesh, a chemist, interested in my experience of LSD. We smoked charass together and went up to sleep on the flat roof in the moonlight. As I unfurled my sleeping bag, a cockroach scuttled out and I went to squash it under my sandal. Ramesh cried out "Don't!" So, I let the bug scuttle off, I didn't kill it.

"Do you eat them?" he asked surprised, as if that might possibly explain my intended act of violence.

I was ashamed to have acted so unconsciously, especially as I had been professing deep interest in Hindu spirituality. I apologized for offending my host. Ramesh replied *Tat tvam assi.* He translated in archaic English, *That thou art.* I remembered you quoting William Blake, *For every living thing that lives is holy.*

Cockroach! Kill! It made me see how culture shapes the way we react to things. Now I regarded the cockroach with newfound respect as the embodiment of life-force just like myself. Perhaps I had been a cockroach in a past life. Perhaps I had saved myself from returning as one in the next. Perhaps I was a cockroach dreaming I was Sam. In a state of some confusion, I fell asleep under the full moon.

In my journal I wrote:

In my dreams I am having the strangest sensations—a power filling this body— in one I was in the path of a train—my body was in a trance and first there was fear, so fast came the train. But then my whole body went rigid, my mind spun away—the force I surrendered to and just in time you led me from the path of the train and I woke. Flies licking my feet.

According to my journal, at 7.30 am Ramesh took me to a garage on the road out of the city. Apparently, due to some festival there would be no traffic for days. This was not a good omen, but Ramesh gave me fifteen rupees, bananas and a pot of honey.

Feeling once again that I had inherited the world and Lord Krishna would provide, I ate the bananas and settled into the garage world in a state of yogic detachment. I put my honeypot on the shelf above the bench I was sitting on and then observed a column of ants circumnavigating the room to feast on my diminishing golden desserts. This appeared as a parable addressed to me. I had once seen a woman carrying a basket of fish on her head. She was going to the market and was totally unaware that a crow had swooped down and swooped off with a fine fish in its beak. This was India. If you could not keep your possessions under your eyes they'd be gone.

It was all Lila, the play of the gods.

Seeking to maintain my state of equanimity, I ceased watching the hungry ants and read from a page of the Bhagavad Gita that Tineke had given me. What it said was ominously relevant.

After gaining transcendental consciousness by the inward stroke of meditation, the mind comes out to engage in activity. The process of repeatedly gaining transcendental consciousness and then engaging in activity results in making permanent the state of enlightenment.

This I fully intended to do, though time had become as viscous as honey whilst I sat in the garage waiting for a ride and I began to feel like a bug trapped in amber.

On the second day: *a man took me to his home and some ten people filled the room to hear me speak, as a penniless European seeking Lord Krishna is something of a novelty.*

Looking back from fifty years in the future I am astonished to see that my experience in the Gita Temple had already created another self, the wannabe spiritual seeker with accompanying followers. I was already imagining a cave in Himalaya. The trickster inside me had taken control of my life-narrative and relished the notion of becoming a guru.

Back in the garage my meditative calm was interrupted by the noisy intrusion of a crowd of 'women' who came to greet me, *neither women nor men, in long dresses and headscarves, gold-toothed, tall, muscular.*

It appeared that they wanted me to go with them. But there is no mention of this in the journal. Perhaps they were Krishna's Gopis and they had come to see me because of my newly professed spiritual kinship as a fellow worshipper of Krishna, who would surely join them in the sacred dance of Spring. Somehow, I resisted the temptation and must have been relieved that night when: *a lorry calls. It is taking me to Pali.*

I ended the day's entry with the following lines:

So much is given me —the bounty of the Lord is beyond reckoning.

The Lord's bounty was so beyond reckoning that no trace of it was recorded in my journal apart from the legend above.

DAY FORTY-SEVEN

Come in number Six. Don't say you're not a number! We already know you are a free man, but you are locked in the cell of your coma. Escape your sentence. Open your eyes. Open your ears. Follow the words. Find your way back home.

Back to my own journey back home.

Time in Eternity's embrace.

Traces of the Holi Festival

For in and out, above, about, below,
'Tis nothing but a Magic Shadow-show,
Play'd in a Box whose candle is the Sun,
Round which we Phantom Figures come and go.

Rubaiyat of Omar Khayyam. Translator Edward FitzGerald.

My uncle had taken the Rubaiyat with him to Burma in the Second World War to fight the Japanese. He returned with the Rubaiyat, malaria and a hatred of all things east of Dover. My father gave it to me before we set off on our journey to the East. The quotation comes in my journal above the following impressions:

The men of Rajasthan wear shirts of many pleats—maroon, buttercup—yellow turbans, brilliant orange. The women, silver bangles on their ankles, long dresses, many-patterned.

Camels hump carts
Elephants are huge
Peacocks are magnificent
Eagles of dawn
Boulder-strewn hills, dry rivers

In the dawning light, I noticed:

Colours on clothes, faces, hands. I even saw a purple dog.

In Pali even the statue of Pandit Nehru is multi-coloured.

Holi the Festival of Colours: bands, fire-crackers, laughter, painted people, walls, dogs, cats.

At that time, all I saw were the colours left in the festival's wake. What had happened here? I had no idea that these impressions would lead me to write an Honours thesis in Anthropology fifteen years later, entitled *The Miraculous Properties of the Abominable.*

The police ask apologetically for my passport ... take me to the Jaipur Golden Transport Co. The manager wishes me to be his guest until the truck leaves for Jaipur, this afternoon.

In the cab an old man with meaning-void eyes shouts, shakes my hand, forces a cigarette on me, is generally rowdy, sounding the claxon regularly, shouting at girls, shouting at cyclists, shouting all over.

He wants me to give him an English passport.

Desert lands, where the rain comes once in two years; drinking water is slightly saline.

It tasted like piss, I felt compassion for the people who had to drink it.

flat-topped houses, like in Iran and Afghanistan
desert light

falling on each goat
and blade of grass, each smoothen boulder
an ulcer in the mouth
cold sores and the bite of every insect between here and Ahmedabad.

I am obviously having difficulty in maintaining the state of yogic detachment I experienced in the Krishna temple.

We reach Ajmer —and the old man leads me to an ashram. There is an Italian and an English girl staying there. I stay too. With much hand shaking and more shouting the old man says goodbye.

The girl has been in India for four years. In the last days of Holi, she has danced in the temple at Jaipur.

I think I was envious. I called her a girl, this brave young woman, and I was still a boy with an extended childhood.

I make obeisance to Hanuman the Monkey god, ringing a bell and raising my hands to a red stone, coloured with silver and shiny papers.

For a lapsed Roman Catholic this was apostasy.

We ate roti, take paan, break a chillum—Boom Shankar!

My Christian Brother teachers would have been horrified at the notion of consuming 'sacred intoxicants!' in a heathen setting, 'a temple!'

The temple keeper wishes to train me: take me to Agra to see his guru, for me to take him to England.

I think he fancies me too.

I neglected to write that he entreated me to sleep with him and that I had to politely refuse, for I was set on enjoying the company of my fellow guests.

In the morning:

Priests with white robes—long black hair fine beards—of which they are very proud.

Bells, gongs, drums, mantra.

I found the combined effects uplifting and as the sun arises:

I walk in the desert. The priest chases me with a chillum—but gives up.

And I am picked up by some merchants in a black car—bombing along to Jaipur, the Pink City through ethereal deserts that pierce your foot with thorns.

DAY FORTY-EIGHT

Morning has broken! Hear the host of birds rejoicing! A mob of cockatoos is already besieging the seed-laden palms and showers of palm nuts are plonking on the shed's tin roof.

But back to the past. After a session of hypnosis with Dr Pendrill, I've been able to recall memories that I had repressed for half a century.

Moksha

There was something familiar about the old man who shook me awake as I was lying in the Lakshmi Hotel in Jaipur. I had spent some of my remaining seventeen rupees on a night here. If I coloured his snowy hair brown, added some teeth and shaved his beatnik goatee, I was looking at me. His hair was rainbow-hued, his face too and all his white garments, all the way down to the bottom of his white dhoti.

He dabbed a smudge of some red paste in the centre of my forehead, saying, "This *bindu* in tantra is an identification with *Kundalini*, the creative energy within. It represents the primordial seed of the cosmos, the creative matrix. It now marks your forehead where *samadhi* is experienced and the equivalence of microcosm and macrocosm is realised".

I had no idea what he was talking about.

He fed me Holi festival foods, dates and parched millet, and made me wash it down with a glass of *bhang lassi* saying, "This is a preparation made from cannabis which, according to legend, sprouted when Amrita, divine nectar dropped from heaven".

"On this day vegetarians may eat meat, tea-totallers may drink alcohol. Men, women and even children drink *bhang lassi*. Welcome to *Lila*, the Play of the Gods. You'd better get dressed". I should have realised then as I looked in vain for my clothes. There was only a sari that could have graced a *devadasi*, a temple dancer.

I objected, saying, "I can't go out like that!"

"But it's play. The full moon of Holi is peak period for the return of the repressed: the lunatic tide is at full. Marking the end of dark tamasic winter and the beginning of spring, it is a festival of reversal, transgression, disorder, ritual defilement and purification, renewal and regeneration.

In Holi sometimes women become men and men become women. The highborn mingle with the lowborn. Everything is reversed, inverted. Wives beat their husbands. Servants are master. Masters are servants". With his words in my ears and with kohl on my eyelashes, I dressed in a sari as a Gopi, a devotee of Krishna. He gave me a round mirror and said, "If you look in this you will see the face of God or ... the Goddess."

I looked divine.

My visitant raised an eyebrow and declared, "The British generally regarded Holi as an obscene and depraved saturnalia, a sentiment shared by Hindus of a puritanical ilk".

He gave me a flute and said, "Play". I said I didn't know how. He said, "Put your lips here and blow and let your fingers open and close the holes". Amazingly the flute played itself as my fingers danced to turn my breath into sound.

He said I was ready.

Going to the open window he stepped out and hung in the multi-coloured cloud, three floors above the clamorous street. He beckoned for me to follow.

After ensuring my sari would not unravel and holding my flute out in front of me, I flew beside him down the street above the heads of merry-making men, women and children, sacred cows, dogs, cats and statues, everything and everyone covered in the cloud of floating colours.

See how the highborn and the lowborn castes commingle in a sudden democratic flush of bhakti, devotion.

Samadhi is the goal. Sameness. Individual awareness dissolves into the great Whole, spontaneous religious ecstasy, the unio mystica.

A barrage of popular songs from films blasted from a battery of loudspeakers.

Despite the din, the words of my elder self spoke in my head like the commentary of a tourist guide heard through earphones.

Holi's multi-coloured besprinklings, abisheka, signify the crossing of an occult threshold, the Victory of the Mother.

More colours fly from countless bags. A rain of Kumkum red powder.

Red is rajasic, the colour of passion, of the emotions, of blood, of the menses, of Shakti, primordial cosmic energy.

Water-pistols drench celebrants in coloured showers, red, green, black, yellow, sometimes of urine, hopefully from the sacred cow.

Gautama, the sacred cow whose urine is purifying!

Holi's yellow-coloured water is considered by some scholars to be a relic of ancient fertility rites in which the priest consumed psycho-active Soma, akin to Amritam, Heavenly Nectar, rendering it safe to be drunk by worshippers in the form of his urine.

Dung flies.

Holi involves play with excremental and menstrual variants, pushing over the boundaries between pollution and purification.

A cacophony of sound came from drums, cymbals, wailing antique clarinets and crackling fireworks.

It is the auditory portion of this sensory input that triggers neural mechanisms underlying trance and ecstatic behaviour.

I saw women wielding mighty phalli and beating submissive men. I saw boys with wooden blocks with rude words engraved and obscene images that were mischievously printed onto the backs of unsuspecting revellers. Some hurled bags filled with coal tar or dung at targets in the crowd. Others beat drums and sang obviously vulgar songs accompanied by coarse gestures. Occasionally all would cry, *"Maharaj land Ki jai!"*

"What did it mean?" I thought and my mentor replied:

Those young rascals, holias, are shouting, "Victory to Lord Penis!" The use of obscenity in language, song and gesture, ostensibly to drive away evil spirits allows a cathartic release of emotion, generally regarded to be therapeutic.

Sandalwood and perfumes grace the air mingled with a tang of heavenly urine and excreta.

It transgresses the boundaries of what is clean and proper. Holi can be regarded as equivalent to the phase of Laya (dissolution) which marks the end of one cosmic cycle and precedes the next. It is the condition of renewal, of cosmic rebirth.

It seemed apposite. I only had a few rupees and was thousands of miles away from home. Now I was wearing a soaking and see-through sari, smelling of patchouli and cow piss (I hoped) and flying with my elder self who had become a pundit.

No consciousness without something to be conscious about. Tat tvam assi! That Thou Art!

I was conscious of a vibrant rainbow-hued phantasmagoria. I wanted to join the dancers in the pandemonium below.

Remember have no fear. Everything you see is Maya, the Dream. Go with the flow. Enjoy.

"Wait!" I cried, but it was too late. He had vanished.

I didn't know how to get back to my hotel and now I was in the middle of a dancing crowd of dye-soaked worshippers. I began to play my flute and dance along too. I couldn't help myself. I was part of a pulsating current of light, colour, sound, smell, people, painted elephants, sacred cows and dogs. People made way for me and clapped in time with my dancing feet. It was amazing. I had never really danced before. Now I was dancing in a sari in wild abandon, a dancing devadasi! They showered me with red powders mixed with glittering talc.

I was really enjoying myself when I kept noticing a man in a Hanuman monkey mask, who seemed to be following me. I broke away from the surging crowd and began to run, only to be caught in the arms of my friends from the garage outside Ahmedabad, the men dressed as women. One said, "Sister, we knew you would join us and achieve *moksha*, release. We knew you would celebrate with us". I wanted to protest that I was not their sister but, looking at my clinging sari, gave up. Instead I asked them if they knew where my hotel was. The Lakshmi Hotel.

"There are a thousand and one Lakshmi hotels!" replied one beauty with a five o'clock shadow. "We shall show you each one and by a process of elimination find yours, hopefully sooner than later."

Everyone found this amusing and soon even I was laughing. They gave me *bhang lassi* to drink and the man in the Hanuman mask appeared. Taking off his mask, I saw it was the priest from the Hanuman temple who had chased after me in the desert outside Ajmer. He offered me his chillum filled with aromatic charass and we shared it with the women.

"Would you rather manifest your devotion by pulling the juggernaut or flying with the gods?" he asked me casually.

Without hesitation I opted for the latter option. Pulling the juggernaut sounded like hard work. I knew I'd made the right choice when a line of straining, sweat-drenched sisters appeared pulling behind them a massive decorated cart designed like a temple and bearing the image of a god with a black face, large eyes and no arms or legs. I noticed with alarm that they were pulling the cart by ropes tied to hooks inserted in the skin of their upper backs.

"The Lord of the Universe, Jagannath!" exclaimed the priest as if that explained everything. "Do you like swings?"

I said that as a kid I loved swings.

"Perfect," he replied. "Wouldn't like you to suffer vertigo." He signalled to my sisters who stepped up and dusted me all over with turmeric like themselves.

"You have been chosen by the Goddess. It is a sacred honour."

I was beginning to wonder what the honour entailed when I was suddenly pinioned by two swarthy sisters and felt sharp pains as hooks were inserted in the skin of my shoulders, my lower back, my buttocks, my calves. I winced each time a hook was inserted and cried *Holi Mata!* with my pierced companions as the hooks were yanked up pulling my flesh into wings behind my shoulders.

"Don't fight it. Go with it," urged my friends. "The greater the pain the more the gain. It marks the level of your devotion. Enjoy!"

Filled with excruciating agonies, the enjoyment side of the equation seemed empty.

A motor started up and six of my sisters and I were hoist into the air, hanging by the hooks in our pliant and yielding flesh. We were held in an ascending circle by ropes dangling from a silver ring in the sky above. My elder-self materialised, flying alongside me. I heard his words in my ears:

You are now part of a living mandala. This mechanism is designed to transform your state of consciousness into an experience of the divine. The swing can be gently soporific like a cradle. More vigorous motions of the swing induce exhilaration, terror or ecstasy. Let your body find a new sense of equilibrium. Let go of your ego!

Easier said than done. My ego had never seemed so attractive. I was crossing more pain thresholds every second and weeping. The crowd below gasped in awe and wonder and let out a mighty cheer. This was cold comfort. My teeth were clenched shut so I couldn't bite my tongue or let out the scream that was building inside me.

You will make seven revolutions, auspiciously following the course of the sun and then go widdershins for an equal number of cycles.

All swinging entails self-surrender. Don't fight it! Find your point of equilibrium, the release of bodily tension. Let go of who you are to become what you might be! Construct a new ecstatic self. Become an aeronaut of the spirit. Fly with the gods!

The ring began to rotate, and we were swung faster and faster. I kept blacking out. I lost count of the number of rotations auspicious or otherwise. I was fighting against vertigo. I vomited *bhang lassi*, dates and parched millet on the psychedelic pandemonium below. Each retch racked my body with tidal waves of accompanying pain as I dangled, jerking up and down in spasm after spasm, all the time being hurled in a circular motion through space and consciousness.

But next instant I was outside of myself. My body had become a bird flying effortlessly above the seething multitude. I was outside of time. I besprinkled those below with red powder and pieces of coconut from a pouch hung from my neck. Filled with exaltation, a beatific grin on my face, my hands joined in prayer, I flew over the world in euphoria beneath the moon of Holi.

This must be *moksha* I thought, but as I said the word a black cloud came over the face of the moon. A flash of lightning came from the cloud, hit the towering crane, incinerating the ropes from which we hung. With the sound of a thunderclap in my ears, I hurled through space.

I woke up on my bed on the third floor of the Lakshmi Hotel, wrapped in a sweaty red sheet. "Wow!" I said and reached for my journal to record my experience. But by the time I found my pen, the dream had faded with the morning light and I was confronted by a monkey who had opened my honey jar and was busy drinking from it. A crow sat on the window ledge and made a derogatory comment.

I thought it said, "*Moksha!*" sarcastically as only a crow can.

When I looked in the mirror, I saw a vermilion smudge in the centre of my forehead but had no recollection of how I had obtained it.

The Day I became Invisible

An opening flower in the palm of a hand
the bloom of cosmic consciousness.

From my window in the Lakshmi Hotel, I saw the pink buildings of Jaipur. I watched monkeys exploring rooftop avenues. I had been told by a fellow traveller that when in Jaipur, I should visit the nearby Amber Palace. I knew I had to return for the Delhi train that evening and hoped to get on without a ticket. I couldn't afford it but I did have enough money for a bit of sightseeing. I didn't realise that it was going to be a day of revelations:

First the valley with its ancient fortifications along the hilltops.

The palace with its mirror rooms and marble screens.

In my journal I recalled a view from a window:

Down in the valley elephants hose themselves in the lake, a camel train passes on the road—eagles soar, monkeys climb.

I dream the dream of life. I am my memories. No, I am what I am this instant.

There is no mention in the journal of what happened next, but I recall making my way down many steps from the palace back to the road and at one point stopping to take in the magnificent view: lake, elephants, camels, monkeys, eagles, the fairy tale palace. Boom Shankar! I made an offering to Shiva with the last of my ganja. I'd bought it in Poona when I'd changed some of my travellers cheques for rupees. I began laughing in wonder, imagining that I'd stood in this spot centuries before, in another body, in another life.

Then I remember walking through a bustling street and seeing a bearded man in white clothes coming towards me, holding something in the palm of his hand and laughing in amazement as if it were the secret of life. He caught my eye and I started laughing too. He was holding a flower. And I could see that he knew I understood. We were both in the timeless zone.

I recall arriving at the station that evening and willing myself to be invisible as I walked between two ticket inspectors at the entrance to the platform.

In my journal I recorded:

Caught the Delhi train at 7.26. Arrived in Delhi 13 hours later—200 miles.

Now I was on my way home.

DAY FORTY-NINE

I'm not sure if I should be saying this to you, but this could be one of the last of my early morning greetings. The virus I told you about has been claiming lives and hospital beds are in short supply. They aren't saying it's about freeing up beds but there has been more discussion about whether to turn off your life-support. You've never liked making quick decisions about urgent matters, but if you're going to wake up, this is a good time. The forty-ninth day. We still have connections to make, man, and I need you here.

I've got more revelations to read to you. It'll blow your mind.

The Superior Person

My treatment with Dr Pendrill is pushing away that black dog and the weight is lifting. All those untold aspects of the past are weaving back into my life narrative, creating new life-enhancing meanings. Using my journal as a source has focused me on its *lacunae*, its gaps. She says that *the story lies behind the lines and in what is not said as much as what is actually said*. At first, I thought it was crazy, but now I see the truth of it.

Like I said, when I first met her, I knew there was something familiar about her, but I couldn't figure out what. Sometimes I'd seen a flash of humour behind her penetrating analytical eyes, suggesting that she'd seen behind my façade and was playing me along. Now something has shifted, a new photo on top of her desk. It drew my eyes straight away: coconut and cashew palms, golden sands. Goa! A much younger Dr Pendrill was standing next to someone we know, the 'Superior Person'! I couldn't believe my eyes. The couple were outside the Casa Bar on the beach. You know the place. We fell in love with the owner's lovely daughters who appeared all dressed up as sprites for carnival one day.

Then I remembered where I'd seen her, Calangute beach of course, arising like a goddess from the foaming sea. The pale moon of her face, the blazing dreadlocks, the saffron robe, the eyes that looked into my soul. Hermaphrodite! Could it really be her ... him? Dr H Pendrill with her cropped snowy hair and look of ironic detachment magnified through her owlish glasses. I felt too embarrassed to bring up the subject of our first encounter. Maybe it was all in my imagination.

When I asked Dr Pendrill who her companion was, she answered *Tathagatta*. Ah, yes, so that was his name. I'd intentionally forgotten it, substituting the nickname *Superior Person* in my memory. She'd met him in Upper Dharamsala and travelled to Goa with him. *Tathagatta* was the name given him by a Tibetan Lama. According to her it is one of the Buddha's names. It means *Thus gone*, like a candle blown out. When I told her I'd met the man in the photo and that it was an amazing coincidence that she knew him too, she replied mysteriously that it was no coincidence. I asked why she hadn't told me of her stay in Goa and she replied that I was the one undergoing psychotherapy and she was under no obligation to discuss her private life. She frowned at me in such an exaggerated way, I took it as a sign of encouragement.

I asked her if she too was given a spiritual name. She replied, "*Ananda*, Bliss. Come into my sanctum sanctorum," and led me into a small room off her study. I couldn't believe my luck.

The room was more like a closet. It was filled with statues of many-armed Indian deities and posters of the gods in garish colours. She looked me in the eye and said, "All the gods have their conception in the human imagination, nowhere else. The artists who produced these sculptures and artworks asked the gods to reveal themselves through dreams. These works are the results of their oneiric quest to understand the nature of the Absolute Reality."

She placed a bronze deity in my hands; its right half was male and its left, female. I recognised Shiva, his matted hair adorned with a crescent moon. His half was naked, lean, ithyphallic and covered in ashes. The other half wore a clinging sari, hair well-combed and an earring. She had a full breast, a slim waist, a curvier body and an anklet on her henna-painted foot. Somehow the craftsman had rendered the pairing with harmony and grace and an underlying erotic charm.

"This union of opposites takes us beyond the polarising spell of Maya to the ultimate oneness at the heart of everything. When the inner masculine and feminine meet, there is a state of perpetual ecstasy, *Ananda*."

"If Ananda is your spiritual name, I'm still wondering what the H stands for." I pushed my luck, hoping for more self-revelations from my enigmatic shrink. She laughed and said, "*Hermione*. The daughter of Helen and Menelaus. I am the messenger. But you have to seek within yourself to find the answers, even to my unspoken questions."

She asked me about Tathagatta and I told her I'd thought he was a charlatan. He wouldn't stop proselytising.

"Perhaps you weren't ready for the truth," said Dr Pendrill with a sigh. "You wouldn't be the first ordinary ignoramus to meet an immortal sage and not recognise the fact." I should have been offended, but I'm sure she had mollified her sarcasm with an ironic twitch of an eyebrow.

On the wall of her study was a saying attributed to Socrates, to the effect that an unexamined life is not worth living. So, after our session, I looked in the journal for a reference to the Superior Person, as I'd called him. I hope you're listening, man. I found a mysterious entry with three blank pages after it. It's what is *not* said that is the mystery, as Dr Pendrill had proclaimed. Maybe I'd left them blank on purpose. Had something happened that I couldn't put into words at the time?

In Consaulim some weeks before Bung's arrival, the villagers brought a traveller to our door, thinking we should look after him. I seem to remember that he was dressed in white like a guru. Maybe he acted all *holier than thou*, I don't remember, just that I took a dislike to him. He was German and he had an unfortunate clipped, peremptory accent that made everything he said seem like a command, an order. He wouldn't stop talking and he sounded to me like a stereotypical Nazi with his talk of the Ubermensch, the Overman.

He went on about living in a universe without any meaning and the need to create one's own values and sense of purpose to overcome the herd mentality. Who did he think he was? Zarathustra? You seemed to be fascinated when he began talking about the Bardo, the Gap between lives, the Lord of Death, Buddha realms and Hungry Ghosts *ad infinitum*. I thought he was a phony, a wannabe Lobsang Rampa.

The next morning, we slept in till ten. I must have been resenting his presence. I went to the well to draw water while you made up porridge and tea for breakfast. I let down the terracotta pot a bit too hastily and it swung out and hit the side of the well and exploded in a shower of sherds. Fuming, I hauled up the useless rim and a legacy of bad luck. Maya Mother, I thought. I've broken your pot. We couldn't do without a pot and that meant a time-consuming visit to Margao.

In my journal I recorded, *"A piss-useless day"*.

I've been trying to work out why I was so disgruntled that I told the visitor to go that night. I mean what came over me? Was I jealous of the amount of time he'd been spending with you, spouting his Bardo nonsense? Yes, I probably was jealous. Two's company. We'd been spending our days swimming, watching ethereal sunrises, magical sunsets, the fisher-people in their outrigger canoes, enjoying tropical fruits, pawpaw, coconut and fresh crab and fish and sleeping on the cow-dung floor of that shack by the railway at Consaulim. Was I just grumpy because the pair of you had got through a tola of Manali in my absence? Probably. Why hadn't I remembered what the Ancient Greeks believed, that one should show hospitality to the stranger who might well be a visiting god or immortal?

We smoked more that night and he went on and on that this world we perceived was not the world but our own socially constructed fiction about it. That it was all in our heads: Maya, illusion! That we had to wake up to *Bodhi consciousness*. You let him rave on and on, until the sound of a cockerel crowing made us realise it was nearly dawn. You started making tea and porridge. More of our supplies would feed our freeloader. Sometimes I wished you wouldn't leave these executive decisions to me. It all got too much for me so I told him to cultivate his own garden and not presume that we were spiritual novices. I told him to stop freeloading and leave.

He got up immediately and said, *I leave you with my Maya*, grabbed his bag and was out the door but not before launching a gob of spit at the wall and saying *Shu*! The saliva hung there in the flickering light of the candle. Then he was gone. Or should I say, *Thus gone?*

The candle flickered out.

Lazarus

"... *Thus gone?*". Your eyes are blinking open and you are staring at the web of drips, electrodes and tubes attached to your body.

Holy Moly! Welcome back, man! Don't try to move. Just relax. The nurse will be with you soon. Just hang in there. How are you? How's it going?

I'm remembering how to breathe again. It's quite important. Talking, that's something else. I'm here hearing words coming out of my mouth. Here? Hearing? It's like I'm being spoken.

And I can only just hear you, man. Did you enter the Luminosity? Did you see the Light?

*Give me a break. Your questions are buzzing inside my skull like demented bluebottles. I didn't only **see** the light, I **was** the f-ing ineffable, all right. Maybe I should go back there.*

Oh, no, man, I'll shut up, I'll shut up.

Good. It's your turn to listen. Those words you said, "Thus gone", opened my eyes. Tathagatta, our guest, left us with his Maya. We've been living under an illusion. This bed I'm lying in. You on your veranda in Kuranda, your hosts of birds, your flying fox, it's all in our heads, man.

Far out! You can't be right. You're spinning out, man.

Still that Doubting Thomas! That's what your mother always called you. You wouldn't recognise truth if it was right under your nose.

Don't get all worked up! Forty-nine days in a coma has addled your brains and stolen your capability for rational thought. Comas can result in memory loss. Can you remember what you were doing when you went into a coma?

Meditating.

I never thought meditation was an extreme sport. Who ends up in ICU from meditating? Were you breathing in that datura pollen? I warned you about that.

Only a sniff or two.

Oh, that'd do it. So what happened?

I gradually slowed down my breathing until I found myself outside my body. I could see myself sitting beneath the angel's trumpet. I felt an electrical current pulsing. I knew I could be anywhere just by thinking of it. A wind picked me up, its rushing noise filling my ears. I was swept into darkness. There was no solid ground. I thought I'd died but incredibly I knew what to do. I was in the Bardo, between life and death. Tathagatta had told me to have no fear. Whatever happened, however terrifying the visions, everything I experienced were projections of myself, man, my own anger and confusion. My very own psycho-dramady. I had to escape from my own box.

You brought your soapbox back with you.

You're not listening, man.

I am, I am. I'm all ears. And I need a whisky. I'll drink to your health. Slange. Of course, I know all about it. I've read the book. Did you meet any Fierce Buddhas? The Lord of Death? Hungry ghosts?

Hungry ghosts? Plenty of them. I've been feeding them forever. You're one of them. Never satisfied. Always want another one. Eyes bigger than your tummy.

Now you're sounding like your old self. That's a good sign. So, you've been turning your nightmares into agents of enlightenment. What's the secret?

I let go.

Did the veil of Maya drop away? Did you lose yourself in the Absolute?

When the inside and outside of the box are exactly the same, there is no box. It's a flow, just one. I was limitless. My breath was the sky.

Far out. That's *moksha* release. If it's so good, why did you leave it? Why aren't you still riding a wave on the Sea of Luminosity?

Because I heard a mosquito whining in my ear and knew I had to come back for you, man. Just a glimpse of that Luminosity can feed you for years. You can't live in that state, though, it's impossible. You need a sense of I-ness if you want to survive. Even if it's just a useful fiction. Our lives depend on our fictions. Words are the bricks of my prison and the feathers of my wings.

I found myself standing on a precipice and I stepped knowingly into the void, floating, floating, floating, shouting out, "I'm dreaming! I'm dreaming! I'm free! I'm free!" I floated down and suddenly found myself in a room.

Looking around, I see I'm in your house in Kuranda. There is no sign of you. In the kitchen dirty cups and plates fill the sink and empty whisky and beer bottles surround the overflowing bin. In the bedroom the bedding lies half on the floor and clothes are strewn everywhere. I find myself tut-tutting like your gecko as I look at the mess. Books and papers on every shelf and table. I begin finding your little gods and immortals, your leprechauns and voodoo dolls all over the place, hidden at the back of the cupboard, behind the books on the shelf and under the table all covered in dust and webs.

One by one I begin picking them up, blowing and brushing away the signs of your neglect.

I keep hearing that monotonous whine and as I focus on it, I hear words and sentences that are meaningless, until I realise they are a bridge to the world I'd left behind. I want that world. I want sunlight, starlight, moonlight. I want the wind. I want trees. I want my white book and a pencil. I want whisky. I want women. I want dope. I want everything. Too much, or not enough!

I follow the sound, come upstairs from your bedroom and there you are sitting on your veranda, reciting from a manuscript. The words are coming from you. The words that hold the key to my earthly identity. I come up behind you and see that you are reciting to someone on your phone. Someone who doesn't look in a good place. In hospital, in fact. I stare at the comatose patient and see that it is me.

And when you say the words, "Thus Gone," I watch myself blink. But when I open my eyes, I am staring at you on a screen at the bottom of my bed. Freaky as! I've just come out of the Bardo! I can see it all. Time past and time future are present in this moment. None of this is real, man. We are living out a dream. When you kicked out our visitor, he left us with a curse, Maya. Our lives have been a convincing illusion. I came back for you. I couldn't remain in the Luminosity and leave you behind in Maya.

Too much, man. I've always seen you as a bodhisattva. But I'm happy here on my veranda. I'm kind of attached. I love my birds and bats. And I've got obligations. Have to pay my rent tomorrow.

Holy shit! I thought you were a free man, a rolling stone. You've picked up a heap of moss.

I have to see my GP tomorrow too and get the results of my blood test. And I haven't bought a Lotto ticket yet. This could be my lucky week.

Sounds great. I see you're a sucker for punishment.

Look at my crystals on the table. I've been collecting them for years. Can't abandon them. This place is in a real mess. Can't leave it for my kids to clean up. God knows what they'll find.

Leave your baggage from the past in their hands. Let it go.

But I've got an unopened bottle of Famous Grouse beckoning from the kitchen shelf and I've cooked myself a far-out curry for tonight. Just have to warm it up.

Hungry ghost number One as usual. You only seek to satisfy your appetites. No sense of adventure. You might miss your dindins.

But these stories I've been writing. I've been putting them out there on Facebook and my profile has never looked so good. Keep getting these dings throughout the night and an avalanche of heart emojis from glamorous avatars. Man, I've just become a limerent entity. If you come back to this present, you'll see your profile has risen exponentially. Everyone wants to know about the West Coast Sculptor in His Coma. You've already attracted young female admirers in Oz. You're glimmering all over. You're a celebrity, man. Publishers will be scrambling to get their hands on our book, *The Other Shore*. Your woodcarvings are going to become national heritage. We've got it made.

Bullshit! You've sold your soul to the devil, to Mammon. You're following that long road to nowhere like a puppet marching to the heartless beat of time. Still ruled by the Machine. No wonder you've been depressed. Cross the soft verge and look through the hedge, man. Check out the everlasting. I've come to take you with me. Back to Consaulim. Back to that night. I know the way.

But how? Fifty years have gone by. We've changed. Will we remember all this? How can we turn our backs on everything we've learned?

You're always saying that we know no more now than we did back then, so what's there to lose? If we forget it, the future will be new to us. If the lives we've lived are our fate, then going back isn't going to change anything.

You mean we'll live through everything all again? Make the same mistakes? If we do anything different the whole future will change. Have you thought of that?

Maybe we can promise to always remind each other of our search for meaning. Maybe we can be just a wee bit wiser. Maybe you won't abandon me when things get tough.

I've already told you how sorry I was about that. But you can't just turn back the clock.

Maybe not in Queensland, but in Scotland we turn it both ways every year. No one bats an eye, an eyelash or an eyelid, unless they're glaikit like you.

Just be serious, if you can. Time is like an arrow heading into the future and we're riding on it.

You can't have it both ways man. You usually harp on about the circularity of time, the eternal return, the yearly cycle of the seasons, the motions of a clock. You are contradicting yourself, changing your tune to suit the occasion.

I'm just being flexible. We all can hold incompatible ideas at the same time.

Okay, have it your way. You've already had your three score years and ten, man. Your ETA might be closer than you think. You might step on a taipan or go flying off the range. You might already have some biological timebomb ticking away inside. Who knows?

Actually, Time is like a ball of string. It keeps on unravelling. We just don't know how much yarn we've got left.

And that virus out there lurking in the shadows. I know you've got a thing about never turning back but look at 'reality'. At our age we can be carried off by a cough and a cold. It's nearly winter here, man. I don't want to be in that lockdown you've been droning on about.

I want to go back, do it all again. Be tumbled by those turquoise waves, wash up on those squeaking sands. I want those virgin highs! Don't you? Or are you yearning for the cold comfort of the grave? Have you forgotten who you are?

Dr Pendrill described us both as *Puer Aeturnus*, Eternal Youths. She said that for the pair of us, our time in Goa, particularly in Consaulim, was a time of transformation, a sudden sense of being in the world, of enlivenment. This sense being so overwhelming that our memories forever return to it as some golden age in which we are forever young. We are in denial of our own mortality. She summed up by saying it is as if the life we are now living is provisional, not the real thing. We are caught in the pull of the Eternal Return back to the source of our awakening.

But man, your shrink has been bringing you back to that time on purpose. She has another agenda. Maybe she wants to meet you back there.

If you don't let go of your comfort zone on the veranda, you'll always regret this lost opportunity. And I can see from the glimmer in your eye you'd love to meet up with your shrink as she was then. What are you waiting for?

You just have to let go! Leave your black dog behind and come with me. You can also abandon your glasses, your dentures, your gout medication and forget your next blood test. Go on, say it, "Too easy man!"

I know the way back to that shack by the railway track. I know the way back home. You have to recite this seed mantra to activate your chakras. It's the Mool mantra. It's a way to escape from your box. Put a foot into the light. Close off your ear with your right thumb and recite the mantra:

> *Satnam I am truth*
> *Truth is my essence*

I have to keep you calm, at least until the nurse arrives. I'll humour you. "Too easy man!" I'm mirroring you and closing off my ear with my right thumb. I'm chanting the Mool.

THE SOUND OF ONE HAND CLAPPING

The door is slamming behind the Superior Person, the candle spluttering out, leaving us in the dark. The coconut-shell candleholder is erupting explosively with hissing, spitting snapping sparks, bursting suddenly into flames, lighting up the room.

"What the ...?"

"Far out man!"

"I heard the sound of one hand clapping."

"I heard it too."

We are both looking at the wall as a gecko is coming out of nowhere and gobbling the gob of spit left by our departing guest.

"Too much!"

You start pouring the tea, "If you want some porridge, you'll need to wash the bowls".

I am sipping my tea slowly. I'll have to go to the well to draw some water, fill the new pot.

The dawn's first glimmer is in the sky. The palm leaves are clattering in a wind off the sea. The cockerel lets out another cry and Vasco the pig is hanging around the toilet, waiting for a feed and grunting in anticipation. The camp dogs are howling one after another and then in unison. The crows are adding their caustic commentary.

Thinking of Mother Maya, with the utmost care I am lowering the pot into the well and letting it slowly fill. And now slowly, slowly drawing it up. It mustn't start swinging or it will implode with a pop as it hits the side. I've learned my lesson.

ACKNOWLEDGEMENTS

The Ancestors. Yours and mine. Without them we'd be nothing.

Parents: Hae Bear and Pig's Dad shared a love of words and a house of books.

My grandfather, Pop, told me horror stories when I was six. He'd been a pilot in the Royal Flying Corps, hit an officer and been court-martialled. He'd lived with lice and rats in the trenches and been gassed. This last fact accounted for his survival. He was lucky to return to Blighty for convalescence. If he'd stayed with his pals, the odds are that my story would never have been written. He taught me that what appears as bad luck can turn into its opposite and vice versa. When my grandfather heard of my journey east, he asked me why on earth I wanted to know what an Afghan tribesman had for breakfast. But he sent me thirty pounds when he heard my money had been stolen in India.

Mr Frank Hughes my English teacher who led me through *The Wasteland* and without knowing it pointed me to the East. He wrote to me in Goa about our odyssey and quoted Eliot on the end of all our explorations.

Harry Pepp, another teacher who opened up the world for me by revealing the illuminating perspectives of foreign filmmakers and accepting me into his family, not as a student but as a friend. He too wrote to me in Goa, offering to send money if I needed it. I didn't take him up on it. Perhaps I was ashamed to have been spending my dwindling fortune on offerings to Shiva.

Professor Elizabeth Grosz, who had me on the edge of my seat as she revealed the world we thought of as real, as a construction, an ideological fiction.

This story *The Other Shore* has its origins in friendship and a shared concern about the nature of reality. My thanks go to you, Phillip Ashman, for allowing me to appropriate your artwork for this picaresque true fiction. Without you there would be no story. Your encouragement has inspired me, and our ongoing communication has influenced its outcome. You are the Friend that Rumi talks about.

Any evidence of higher order thinking, such as logical sequencing, meaningful plot development, ironic juxtapositionings and sense in general, can be attributed to my editor, Dr H Ramoutsaki. You showed me that less is best. Your insight into literary craft has shorn my tale of its pompous academic hair, trimming off clichés and empty air, reminding me of commas and full stops, administering Occam's razor to my empty philosophical posturings and keeping me on track. You did your best, but I probably slipped a few breaches beneath your scrutiny for which the responsibility is all my own. I feel like Theseus and you are Ariadne, showing me the way through the labyrinth of my own mind. You say, no way. I'm not Theseus and you'll never be Ariadne, not for anyone. Sometimes your words have entered my discourse and I don't know who is the author, whose self is talking.

Han Shan, Rumi, William Blake, Nietzsche, Walt Whitman, E.M. Forster, T.S. Eliot, the Beatles, Chogyam Trungpa, Phillip Ashman. And you Mnemosyne. Memory. Mother of the Muses.

All of you in me, shaping my thinking and colouring my words.

Boom Shankar!

ABOUT THE AUTHOR AND THE ARTIST

(Image: Tim Quinn)

Artist, Phillip Ashman, on the left, looking determinedly into a vista of the future and storyteller, Michael Quinn, nonchalantly bemused.

Our long friendship has made this collaboration possible.

Phil lives on the west coast of Scotland and makes mead and wine from the honey of the bees and fruits of his garden. He cultivates bonsai trees and strawberries. In the winters he carves on wood. He immerses himself in the sea in warmer seasons. All year round he provides counselling services to the community, who open up to him over the course of several pints of his famous stout. Always the perfect host, he never sits down until the last guest is out of the door or under the table. He has been mistaken for Rembrandt Junior and a Celtic shaman. No words can sum him up.

Michael lives in a rainforest on the east coast of Australia. He works with the First People of that place to keep alive their language and storytelling traditions that reach back into the last ice-age. The wisdom within the Storywaters is life-enhancing, in harmony with the world we live in, based on a sharing of resources and dutiful care-taking of the environment, its flora and fauna. Any more you would like to know about Michael can be guessed, perhaps, from his fictions.